Beryl Fletcher has published short stories, four novels and a volume of memoir *The House at Karamu* (2003). Her first novel *The Word Burners* won a regional (Pacific, South East Asia) Commonwealth Writer's Prize for Best First Book in 1992.

Her novels take as their theme the re-writing of established power structures, particularly those of the patriarchy. She has been awarded two writers in residence in the USA (1994 and 2005) and two in New Zealand. Her work has been translated into German and Korean. In 2009 she was appointed the Pan-Commonwealth judge of the Commonwealth Writer's Prize.

OTHER BOOKS BY BERYL FLETCHER

The Word Burners (1992/2002)
The Iron Mouth (1993)
The Silicon Tongue (1996)
The Bloodwood Clan (1999)
The House at Karamu (2003)

BERYL FLETCHER
Juno & Hannah

Spinifex Press Pty Ltd
504 Queensberry St
North Melbourne, Victoria 3051
Australia
women@spinifexpress.com.au
www.spinifexpress.com.au

First published by Spinifex Press 2013
Copyright © Beryl Fletcher, 2013

All rights reserved. Without limiting the rights under copyright reserved above, no part of this publication may be reproduced, stored in or introduced into a retrieval system, or transmitted, in any form or by any means (electronic, mechanical, photocopying, recording or otherwise) without prior permission of both the copyright owner and the above publisher of the book.

Copying for educational purposes
Information in this book may be reproduced in whole or part for study or training purposes, subject to acknowledgement of the course and providing no commercial usage or sale of material occurs. Where copies of part or whole of the book are made under part VB of the *Copyright Act*, the law requires that prescribed procedures be followed. For information contact the Copyright Agency Limited.

This is a work of fiction. Names, characters, places and incidents either are the product of the author's imagination or are used fictitiously. Any resemblance to actual persons, living or dead, events, or locales is entirely coincidental.

Cover design by Deb Snibson
Cover photo © Simon Tarrant
Typesetting by Claire Warren
Printed by McPherson's Printing Group

National Library of Australia cataloguing-in-publication data:
CIP
Fletcher, Beryl, 1938–
Juno and Hannah
ISBN 9781742198750 (pbk)
ISBN 9781742198705 (eBook pdf)
ISBN 9781742198774 (eBook Kindle)
ISBN 9781742198798 (eBook ePub)
1. New Zealand fiction
NZ823.2

For my daughter and my granddaughter.

Chapter 1

Some floods are silent, slow moving, tone deaf to the possibility of fugue and counterpoint. For weeks, the rain had held a polyphonic conversation on the galvanised iron roofs of the settlement. Sometimes the rain sang a lullaby, but when the wind came roaring up the valley pushing a wall of water before it, the roofs reverberated like a kettle drum. There was talk about the rising level of the river. Abraham announced that they faced the prospect of becoming completely cut off from their supply route to Piopio.

Hannah was not concerned. Wet or fine, her tasks in the community remained much the same. The only problem was Juno. She hated to be cooped up inside and Hannah had to devise extra activities in order to keep her apart from the others.

One afternoon, the rain drifted away. At first the change was so slight that Hannah did not notice the pale sunlight that was threading through the thin white trunks of the mahoe that grew in profusion outside the kitchen windows.

Juno came to tell her about the return of the light. 'I want to go outside,' she said.

Hannah took her hand and told her to be quiet. She led Juno into the washhouse. It was set apart from the other buildings in the settlement. They took oilskins from the coat rack and put them on over their knitted tops and long skirts. They removed their cotton slippers and borrowed two pairs of leather boots from the men's shoe rack. Hannah tied the laces around the outside of Juno's boots to stop them from falling off her tiny feet.

They crept away into the bush. The sodden branches of trees and ferns hung low with moisture and they had to constantly duck their heads to avoid taking a cold shower. Soon, their head scarves were soaking wet and Hannah wrung them out and placed them on a manuka bush in the hope that the sun might gain strength in the late afternoon.

They heard the river roaring below them before they saw it. Hannah helped Juno down the steep track to the swimming hole. The floodwater had eaten away the shallow banks of the place where in summer the women came to wash their long hair in the cool fresh water.

Now, in flood, the once gentle stream was dark and agitated. The weeping willows were half submerged and the swift current tore at their lower branches as if to rip them from the arms of the mother lode.

Juno sat on a flat rock at the edge of the water. She began to remove her boots.

Hannah restrained her. 'No paddling today, too dangerous.'

Juno pointed at one of the willow trees. 'A man down there.'

'What?'

'A man in the water.'

At first Hannah thought that Juno was playing games; she often saw things in the physical world that existed only in her mind. Hannah looked more closely. Yes, there was something caught in an eddy at the edge of the water. A willow tree obscured the view. She walked slowly along the edge of the swimming hole being careful not to sink down into the mud.

Then she saw it. A man lying on his back, half out of the water, trapped by a fallen branch. One arm was stretched above his head displaying a roughened hand with thickened fingers. She took hold of this hand and it was cold and white.

Juno called out. Hannah could not make out her words. Something about a horse. She sounded frightened. Hannah ordered her to stay exactly where she was.

All at once the hand moved. It clung to Hannah's fingers like a disembodied claw.

Hannah grasped the man beneath his armpits and began to pull him clear of the fallen branch. She managed to drag him onto the mud at the edge of the water. She turned his head towards her and saw the face of a stranger. She ripped off his worsted underwear and tucked her skirt up into her waistband. She sat astride his naked body and placed her lips on his. She blew the air into his mouth until she saw his lungs shudder. She turned him on his side and watched him disgorge copious amounts of river water and dark oily clumps of something solid.

She became aware that she was under surveillance. Juno silently appeared at her side. Hannah was about to reprimand her for coming too close when she looked up and saw two men on horseback. They were partially obscured by the regenerating scrub.

She called out to them. 'Help me, please, help me!'

One of the men dismounted and climbed down the rough track. It was Abraham. He removed his felt hat and held it by the brim. He ordered her to release her skirt from her waistband and to leave the body alone. It had nothing to do with them. He covered the man's flaccid genitals with his hat. Juno giggled.

'This innocent child should not be exposed to such sights,'

said Abraham. 'I will ride into town tomorrow for the constable to come with a konaki to retrieve the body.'

'But he is still alive,' said Hannah. 'God in his infinite grace has saved him.'

She arrived back at the kitchen and took off her wet things. She threw lumps of fuel into the fire box of the coal range. There was a pleasant aroma of roasted potatoes and mutton. Abraham came into the kitchen and ordered the women on cooking duty to prepare barley soup and bread for their unexpected guest and to find him some decent clothes. Then send him on his way.

'No,' said Hannah. 'The poor man is too weak to make his way on foot through the bush. He must stay until he has regained his strength.'

Everything stopped except for the rhythmic clanking noise Juno was making by hitting an empty saucepan with a stick. Tap! Tap! Tap!

Hannah would not let it go. 'The man's horse has been swept away in the river taking his saddle packs with him. He has nothing left.'

Tap! Tap! Tap!

Hannah opened the oven door and began to turn the potatoes over with a wooden spurtle. Abraham said for the sake of his sanity would someone please control that child.

Tap! Tap! Tap! Hannah removed the pot and the stick from Juno. The child clicked her tongue and tried to mimic the sound of the stick. Tip! Tip! Tip!

Abraham said that the situation was murky. Jimmy and Conrad had been sent to find the man's horse but after searching the riverbank they had failed to find any trace of the beast. It was becoming clear that the situation required further investigation. There was a suggestion that the man had been sent to spy on them.

Tip! Tip! Tip!

'I am a fair man,' said Abraham, 'and one who adheres to the sacred principles of Christian justice. The stranger is permitted to stay until he has recovered on the condition that before he leaves there will be a hearing. Hannah will have every chance to tell us the truth about the drowned man and how it was that she brought him back to life.'

He turned and left. Juno began to chant 'back to life, back to life' in her copycat voice. Hannah placed a warning finger on her mouth and the child fell silent. The women in the kitchen came out of their collective trance and murmured between themselves. Hannah turned her back on them and finished attending to the potatoes. The heat of the oven blasted her face.

The murmurs became louder and the comments and questions more pointed. Then Sarah stood up from her stool and clapped her hands. 'Be silent,' she said. 'The food will be spoiled with this idle chatter.'

'Her shame is written on her body,' said Augusta. 'There is no need for words.'

'In that case,' said Sarah, 'let there be an end to it.'

The trial was brief and to the point. Hannah denied prior knowledge of Mr Wilfred Cattermole before she saw him washed up on the bank of the swimming hole. She did not understand why she had removed his underclothes. She did not understand why she was able to put the breath back into his body. Someone or something had guided her.

Mr Cattermole was seated in front of Hannah in the meeting room. When he turned his head to look at her, she barely recognised him from the glacial being that had lain beneath her at the swimming hole. He looked relaxed and healthy and his beard was neatly trimmed. He was dressed like the other men; flannel shirt, denim dungarees and a felt hat.

Mr Cattermole was not able to explain what he was doing near the river. His memory had gone, flown away like a paper dart, skedaddled. He can remember leaving Piopio on his horse some time ago and that it is the winter of 1920. After that, it's a blank. No, he does not know Miss Hannah Cooper. Never laid eyes on her before. He didn't even know that this place existed. He would like to know when they had arrived here to take up the land.

'We are not here to answer your questions,' said Abraham. 'You are the trespasser, not us. You must leave today and go back to where you belong. Jimmy and Conrad will take you to the boundary of our land.'

'What was the name of the river that took my horse and almost took me?'

'Our land has its own name and so does the river,' said Abraham.

'By the look of it I reckon it to be a tributary of the Mokau.'

'You will not find us on any map.'

Mr Cattermole stood up. 'Don't bother with an escort. I am well used to the ways of the bush. I can find my way back to Piopio.'

'Go then,' said Abraham. 'There is a package of food and a bed roll outside on the porch. Take them and leave.'

Mr Cattermole turned at the door and doffed his hat at the assembly. He gave Hannah a conspiratorial wink.

She was mortified by this unwanted gesture of familiarity.

Worse was to come. Abraham summoned her to the front of the room and instructed her to face her accusers. Did she not understand the gravity of her actions? She had shown disrespect towards the elders. Her arrogance must be reined in.

'I am loath to do this,' he said, 'but I have no choice. You will be subject to the punishment of internment for the period of one lunar month beginning next Sabbath when the moon is at its lowest point.'

Hannah could feel her body close down. Her legs shook. She tried to hold her head up high and look them in the eye but none would engage her.

Abraham asked the assembly to pray for her soul. Then he read from the book of Samuel in the Old Testament. *Saul said unto his servants seek me a woman that hath a familiar spirit . . . and his servants said to him behold there is a woman that has a familiar spirit at Endor . . .*

The felt hats nodded in approval. Abraham put down his bible and took hold of Hannah's head. She locked her eyes onto his. She forced herself to stay calm. He will not make me cry, he will not . . .

'Learn your lesson from the sacred book,' said Abraham. 'Only God has the right to bring back the dead. Do not enter the dark and dangerous world of the bone-conjuror even if a king himself begs you to do so.'

He went to the door. Sarah was waiting outside.

'Take her now,' he said.

All through the night Hannah sat on her canvas cot next to the open window. She watched the incandescent stars pierce the vast canopy of a sky that deepened from indigo to black. To her, the stars appeared as white hot torches of judgment.

Each hour she removed another garment baring more skin to the air until she was almost naked. She was unconcerned that the other women in the dormitory might open their eyes and see her exposed white flesh. The other members of the community had been forbidden to comment upon her bodily states until the period of internment was over. The women obeyed without question. They did not register her nakedness by the flick of an eye. She might as well have been made of gelatine or isinglass.

She had not comprehended until now the loss that imposed invisibility could bring. Even Juno had looked through her with a strange floating gaze, empty and unfocussed, as if her flesh had vanished and she no longer had the ability or substance to cast even the thinnest of shadows.

The wintry air acknowledged her presence by shrouding her body in an icy cloak that made her shiver. Hannah welcomed the scourging of her flesh. She could offer no explanation for her ability to bring life back into a drowned body. The elders had tried to force her to tell them the truth. She desperately wanted to please them but to do so would force a moral descent into the sin of lying.

She tried to comfort herself by conjuring up a vision of her mother but the fading away of Eleanor's physical presence was almost complete. All that remained was a blurred glimpse of slender ankles disappearing beneath the uneven hem of a long skirt, and once, an ear lobe shedding blood when caught in the clasp of an obsidian earring.

Although Hannah could no longer conjure up her mother's face, she had a clear memory of the musical range of her voice. Her mother loved to tell stories of domestic mishaps that through constant retelling had taken on the power of grand epics.

Hannah wondered how Eleanor would have told the story of the drowned man and the hand clutching at her like a claw.

She tried to visualise her mother taking hold of Mr Cattermole in the cold river water and all at once she saw a clear view of Eleanor's hands fresh from the rigors of the wash tub; one crushed finger nail on her left index finger; a ragged purple scar on the back of her right hand that in a certain light could look like a dog's head or a crude map of Australia.

This unexpected recall of her mother's wounded hands gave Hannah a sense of comfort. Something that had been lost to her since she was a child had been given back. She closed the window and climbed beneath her grey blanket just before the dawn light began to break out behind the hills.

Sarah was the only woman permitted to speak to Hannah during the time of internment. She brought food and brief snatches of gossip when the others were working on their assigned tasks. Hannah did little else except lie on her cot and day dream. When the early morning sky was clear of rain clouds she watched the silhouette of the steep hills emerge with the coming of a new day. She listened to feral roosters serenading the return of the light and the restless sheep dogs rattling their cages. She listened to the sound of the wind sighing through the mamaku tree ferns that held their delicate green umbrellas above the regenerating scrub of kanuka and mahoe.

When the wind changed direction and came from the south it brought cold driving rain that formed rivulets of mud around the buildings. The women brought candles in at night and held them up to the windows so that they could see the depth of the slush outside. Mud was their enemy. Their long skirts became sodden with sticky clay soil as they scampered between the kitchen and dormitory and the children's house. The pulley in the kitchen ceiling was strung with wet washing and the men complained that their shirts and union suits smelled of mutton chops and stewed tea.

When the southerly blew itself out, fog crept up from the river and devoured all before it. Not one leaf moved, not one bird sang. One by one the trees melted away. The fog brought a terrible silence outside her prison that emulated the social death within.

Without work Hannah's sense of time became distorted. The nights were long. After the last candle was extinguished the women who shared this hut with her went to sleep instantly and slept like the dead. It had never occurred to her before that all of them were in a constant state of exhaustion.

The days were difficult to bear. Sarah brought Hannah a slice of brown bread spread with honey for her breakfast. This had to satisfy her until teatime when she received a cup of water, a bowl of cooked vegetables or soup and another slice of bread.

'I'm frightened,' said Hannah. 'Sometimes I forget my name.'

'Hush now,' said Sarah. 'Eat your potatoes and drink your tea.'

'But tea is forbidden.'

'Drink it while it's still hot.'

Hannah gulped a mouthful of tea. 'What colour were my mother's eyes? I am forgetting to remember.'

Sarah gathered up the dishes and put them onto a tray. She hid the empty cup in the front pocket of her apron. 'Don't tell anyone. About the tea I mean.'

'Go now,' said Hannah. 'Your transgression is safe with me.'

Five days before Hannah's period of internment was due to finish, Sarah came early with the bread and honey. She brought the news that Hannah was to be released at once. She had held a meeting with the other women last night about Juno, and this morning the elders had given Hannah permission to resume her normal life.

'Is Juno ill?'

'She has not spoken a word since you were sentenced. All she does is sit and rock and yesterday she began to bang her head against the kitchen door.'

'I must go to her.'

'Eat first, that was the instruction.'

Hannah bolted down her bread. She barely noticed the cup of tea that Sarah had brought for her. She poured some water from her jug into the washbowl and threw handfuls of cold water over her face.

'I tried to stop her,' said Sarah, 'but she would not listen to me.'

'It only makes things worse to argue with her, you know that.'

Sarah's face crumpled. Hannah felt a moment of compassion for her. When Sarah had lost her son Harry in the influenza epidemic she had turned almost overnight into a frail old woman. Her flesh seemed to melt away and her bones became clearly visible beneath her skin. She had fallen back into the interior of her body as if she no longer had a right to live there.

Hannah was not able to comfort her now. It was all she could do to stay upright. Her legs had weakened. But this was a minor discomfort compared with an emotion that was beginning to invade her bones like a slow but insistent poison; resentment against those in authority.

'Don't make any more trouble for yourself,' said Sarah.

'I'm ready,' said Hannah.

Juno was in the small room at the back of the meeting hut

that was designated as a sick bay, a place where ill people could be segregated from the healthy workers. The two iron hospital beds were empty. A small white cupboard between the beds concealed a commode. A shelf holding a collection of medicines was attached to the wall. Bottles of zinc sulphate, quinine, aspirin and friar's balsam stood in neat rows. Lumps of camphor sewn into muslin bags hung from hooks above the shelf.

Juno was standing between the beds. Her brown eyes were small and deep like the glass eyes on a child's soft toy. Her body quivered. She looked ready to run away at a moment's notice.

'I have brought Hannah to you,' said Sarah.

Juno did not respond.

'Maybe it would be better if we went out into the bush,' said Hannah.

'The wind has turned,' said Sarah. 'Heavy rain will soon be upon us.'

'We could go to the kitchen and sit on the settle out of the way of the workers.'

'She is banned,' said Sarah.

'What happened?'

'She threw a bowl of setting cream all over Augusta.'

'I'm so sorry,' said Hannah.

'I shouldn't be telling you this but there's a move underway to get rid of her.'

Hannah was shocked. She hoped that Juno had not heard what Sarah had said. Juno's eyes still held that floating gaze, empty and unfocussed, as if she could not see what was right in front of her face but that did not mean that she could not hear.

Sarah lowered her voice. 'We can no longer afford to keep her. There is talk of sending her to an orphanage in town.'

Juno gave a strange cry and fell to the floor. Hannah crouched down and held her in her arms. Juno began to bang her head against the wooden floor.

Thump! Thump! Thump!

Hannah tried to hold Juno's head upright but the child resisted her. Hannah cried out to Sarah but the old woman had gone.

Thump! Thump! Thump!

Hannah had never seen Juno like this before. She did not know what to do. All she could think of was to hum a tune. A ballad she had once heard swam up into her mind. She had forgotten the words so she sang the melody to the nonsense sounds of da da da . . . da da da . . .

Juno stopped banging her head. She garbled something to Hannah about a terrible noise of coughing, a child gasping for breath. She could see other bad things too; a man's back covered with black spots and a lady with blood running from her nose, down her front, all over her blouse.

Hannah sang da da da again to Juno. She stroked Juno's cheeks and told her not to be afraid. 'Pay no attention to those shades. Snap! Snap your fingers like I taught you to do, walk backwards around a circle, throw salt, anything to put them in their place.'

The room darkened, and soon the rain was pinging off the iron roof like gunshots. Juno asked for a candle. She smiled with delight when Hannah opened the little cupboard between the beds and brought out the stub of a candle and a box of wax vestas from behind the commode. On the cover of the matchbox was a white swan. Inside the box were three matches. Hannah gave one to Juno. She tried to light it by striking the match on the wooden door of the cupboard. Hannah suggested she try it on the sole of her shoe. Juno gave a cry of joy when the match flared up.

'Quickly,' said Hannah. 'Let's throw some light around.'

The candle stub hissed and burned. Juno asked if she could have another match to light with her shoe. Hannah said no. There were just two left in the box. They had to be saved for something more important. Juno asked if she could have the Swan box when it was empty.

'Of course,' said Hannah. 'But first you have to be very brave.'

Juno nodded.

'And you have to promise me that you can keep a really big secret.'

Juno nodded again.

'We are going away, just you and me.'

Juno asked where they were going.

Hannah said that she was not sure yet. She placed the box of Swan vestas and a bottle of aspirin into her coverall pocket. She unhooked a camphor bag from the wall and hung it beneath Juno's camisole to keep her safe from harm. The candle stub spluttered out.

They came out of the sick bay. There was no one in the meeting room. They ran hand in hand to the kitchen porch that provided some shelter against the driving rain. Hannah's legs ached with the unaccustomed movement. She knew then that she must lie low for a few days in order to regain her strength for the journey ahead.

Hannah opened the kitchen door. Augusta was turning out a loaf onto a wire cooling rack. There was a delicious smell of hot bread.

Sarah was stirring a soup pot on the coal range. 'Two drowned rats,' she said.

'Sorry,' said Hannah.

'Dripping all over my clean floor,' said Augusta.

'Sorry,' repeated Hannah.

'You will be, if you don't keep that wretched girl under control.'

Sarah replaced the lid on the soup pot. She asked Augusta to forgive Juno for the incident with the cream. The kitchen ban must be lifted until this wicked storm had blown itself out. The poor child might catch her death.

Augusta did not answer. Sarah took this as tacit consent. She unwound the rope that held the clothesline securely in place and lowered it down from the roof. She plucked a threadbare towel from the pulley and helped Juno to dry her face and hair.

Augusta was knocking down the dough for the next batch of bread. She hit the dough with the side of her hand until it was almost flat then folded it up into smaller rectangles before knocking it down again. Thump! Thump! Thump!

The sound made Hannah nervous.

Juno emerged from Sarah's vigorous rubbing with the towel. Her cheeks were flushed with heat and her eyes glittered. 'Not allowed to tell,' she said. Augusta's busy hands stopped in mid-air above the dough.

'It's just an old tune without words,' said Hannah. 'I told her to keep it a secret.'

'Da da da,' sang Juno.

Augusta resumed torturing her dough. Sarah shook out the damp towel and hung it back on the line. She placed two bowls on the table and filled them with potato and mutton broth. She took a serrated knife and hacked two slices from the hot loaf.

'I need to make sandwiches for the men's lunches from that,' said Augusta. 'Look how you've shredded it.'

Hannah was hungry. She wolfed down the hot meaty soup,

almost scalding her throat in the process. Juno ate more slowly, pausing now and then to repeat Augusta's words you've shredded it, shredded it, shredded it ... until Augusta threw her arms up into the air and walked out of the door saying that she'd had enough, it was more than a body could bear.

Sarah took over the bread-making. She rolled some dough into thin strips and plaited them together to make a decoration for her loaves. Juno asked her if she could make a little loaf. Sarah gave her some dough, a rolling pin, and a tin with holes in the lid to dust the pastry board with flour. Juno soon became engrossed in her task.

'Look at her,' said Hannah. 'It takes so little to keep her happy. The orphanage would break her heart. And mine.'

'We can't carry a non-productive member no matter how much it grieves us.'

'Juno is capable of doing domestic work if someone is there to guide her.'

'There is some resentment against her,' said Sarah.

'Why?'

'For not dying in the flu epidemic when the healthy young ones did.'

Hannah was shocked into silence. It was on the tip of her tongue to ask Sarah if she felt like that over the loss of her son Harry.

Sarah opened the oven door and turned the loaves so that the crusts would brown evenly. She mumbled something about having to accept God's will, like it or not.

Juno had made a mess. The table and the floor were sprinkled with flour. The dough that she had tried to make into a plaited loaf was blackened from constant kneading with her grubby fingers. She asked if her little loaf could go into the oven after the big ones were cooked.

'Of course,' said Hannah. 'And then you can eat it while it's hot.'

'It's fit only for the pig bucket,' said Sarah.

'Pig bucket pig bucket,' cried Juno.

'No,' said Hannah. 'We will smother the little loaf in melted butter and eat it together.'

'Promise?'

'Promise.'

Two nights after the scene in the kitchen Hannah was awakened by something blowing softly into her left ear. At first she thought that a flapping moth had taken up residence inside her head but then she heard a faint whisper. 'Wake up, wake up.' It was Sarah.

'Has something happened to Juno?'

'No, she's sound asleep.'

'Can't this wait until the morning? I'm tired.'

'Sorry,' said Sarah. 'But I need to speak with you urgently.'

Heavy rain was falling. The howling wind performed a series of suspended cadences that never quite developed into a decisive final note. Hannah crept out of the hut and followed Sarah to the kitchen.

Sarah raked the embers in the fire box with the poker. She put some small logs onto the embers and the dry bark on the wood flared up with a hissing sound. She filled the teapot with boiling water from the tap at the side of the range and brought out the milk jug and the jar of sugar from the safe.

'I know that you are leaving,' she said. 'Juno told me.'

Hannah took a gulp of hot tea that almost burnt her gullet. It had been a mistake to trust Juno. She did not understand the necessity for secrecy. The girl had no guile, no artifice and she trusted all adults implicitly.

'For what it's worth,' said Sarah, 'I believe that you're doing the right thing. I have worked out a plan. I've borrowed bed rolls and a pikau for you to take. But you must be careful. Winter time is dangerous in the bush.'

'If they find out that you have helped us you will be punished,' said Hannah.

Sarah poured more tea into her cup. 'You must leave as soon as possible. A man and a lady are coming from the orphanage to take Juno away when the weather clears.'

She went over to the sideboard and retrieved a stained manila envelope from the back of the cupboard. 'Pictures,' she said. 'You will need to take them with you.' She laid out three photographs on the table and placed the candle closer to Hannah.

One photograph was of a shop window displaying men's clothing. The second one was of a young woman dressed in a satin gown with an intricate pleated bodice and the last one was of the same woman, a little older, holding a baby dressed in a sailor suit.

Hannah could not take her eyes off the young woman. The iridescent perfection of her skin glowed through the matt sepia surface with the lustre of pearls.

'Is that my mother?'

'Yes and that's you, dressed as a boy.'

Sarah's hands began to shake. She complained of feeling faint. Hannah fetched a pillow from the linen press and propped her up on the settle.

Someone knocked on the kitchen door. Hannah ignored it at first. It was barely audible above the raging wind playing havoc with a flapping sheet of iron on the roof. The knocking became more insistent. Hannah placed the photographs back into the manila envelope and hid it beneath her night shirt but before she could blow out the candle, the kitchen door opened.

It was Jimmy. He was dressed in dripping wet oilskins and leather boots. He stood in the doorway awkwardly with his sodden hat in his hands.

'It's a filthy night outside,' he said.

Sarah said that she had just suffered one of her turns and that she must keep still for a few moments until the blood came back into her face. Hannah asked him what he was doing here.

'Jimmy is part of the escape plan,' said Sarah. 'He'll take you and Juno to the edge of the bush before first light.'

'It's almost time for me to go and catch Prince and prepare the konaki,' said Jimmy.

Hannah waited until Jimmy had closed the kitchen door behind him before she removed the photographs from her night shirt. She took them out of the envelope and laid them out on the table. The young woman was looking down at the baby in the sailor suit with a look of utter adoration. The baby could not be an image of Hannah when young. To be so loved and then abandoned made no sense.

Sarah looked shrunken and somehow diminished in the flickering candlelight. She offered Hannah some waterproof wrapping to protect the photographs from the rain.

'I should have given you these a long time ago,' she said, 'but I was afraid that you would find them unsettling.'

'You were right,' said Hannah.

Outside, the rain roared like an inland tidal sea. Hannah thought she heard Sarah whisper, please forgive me, but it might have been the desperate sigh of an uprooted tree fern or a drowning animal fighting for a final gasp of air against the power of the storm.

Sarah stood up. 'Come now,' she said. 'My head has settled. It's time for you to leave.'

The konaki proved to be a problem right from the start. Jimmy said little but when he did he surprised Hannah with the coarseness of his language. Some blankety-blank idiot had attached two small wheels to the back of the sledge and they kept getting caught in the low branches of the bush along the track. He rode slowly and cautiously, but every so often he had to dismount from Prince and chop at the vegetation caught in the wheels. He had to shout over the noise of the wind and the rain and the flailing trees. There were no runners on the konaki and if he, Jimmy, ever met the idiot who had taken them off, he would tell him to go to the hot place.

By the time the dawn light appeared the rain had reduced to a dribble and the wind had died down to a mere whisper of its former self. Hannah marvelled at Juno's ability to sleep through the severe jolting of their transportation through the terrible night. But as soon as they stopped, Juno awoke. She sat encased in her blankets with her headscarf pulled down low over her forehead.

Jimmy removed the horse from the shafts of the konaki. Juno slid down the front of the sledge onto the ground. She giggled.

Hannah was annoyed. Jimmy could at least have lifted Juno out of the konaki before he released his horse. She could have hurt herself.

Jimmy tied on a canvas feedbag over Prince's head. The horse snuffled and coughed into his oats. Jimmy said that he would light a fire to make tea and dry out their things. He took some shredded bark and small pieces of paper from his pikau. He fiddled about trying to make sparks with a stick of hardwood and a piece of whitey-wood but the dampness defeated him.

Hannah gave him one of her precious matches. He asked her where she had got it from but she would not tell him.

'Do you know where we are?' he asked.

She shook her head. Jimmy said it was a shame that Hannah had never learned to ride a horse. He could have saddled up one for her and Juno and then they would not be at the mercy of this wretched konaki.

The paper caught fire and she helped Jimmy to place small pieces of bark in a pyramid shape to feed the flames. Soon the fire was well alight and when it had died down Jimmy made a flat area in the middle of the embers to make a nest for the billy. When the water boiled, he lifted the billy out of the fire and placed it on the ground. He removed the lid and threw in a handful of tea. He gave it a vigorous stir with his pig knife.

'Now we must wait for it to steep,' he said. 'Nothing worser than rushed bush tea.'

'I'm hungry,' said Juno.

Hannah opened her pikau and took out a brown-paper parcel. Inside were two honey sandwiches, four slices of thick unbuttered bread and a small wheel of cheese. She offered a slice of bread to Jimmy. He shook his head and beckoned to Juno. 'Got pork hocks in my saddlebag. Come over here and get some meat.'

Juno came closer to the fire. Hannah felt uneasy, not at what Jimmy had said, but the tone of his voice. He kept staring at Juno's face as if he had never seen her before. He tipped up the billy and poured strong dark tea into chipped enamel mugs. Juno wolfed down the chunks of fatty meat and gristle that Jimmy hacked from one of the hocks. She wanted to know how the pig walked after someone took its legs away.

Jimmy laughed. 'Oh aren't you the funny one, a breath of fresh air you are.'

Hannah's unease deepened. He was a few years older than her and had always seemed a quiet young man, respectful of his uncle Abraham and the other elders. He was gentle with the farm animals and, unlike some of the other men, never whipped his dog or kicked the house cows.

Now, it seemed as if he was playing a different game. He had taken on an air of authority over them, an ownership. Hannah wondered why he was helping them when he knew of the possible consequences of his action.

The bush was wet and dripping with moisture. The horse had dozed off with the feedbag still attached to his head. Jimmy put some more fuel on the fire.

'Time is moving on,' said Hannah. 'Perhaps we should resume our journey.'

'Soon,' said Jimmy.

Then he told them a story of a boy and a girl who fell in love and who had run away from the settlement. They had become lost in the bush.

'Were they punished?'

'They died of cold and hunger. But their ghosts live on in the bush. Listen, can you hear what they are doing?'

Hannah saw a look of panic on Juno's face at the mention of ghosts. 'Come Juno,' she said. 'Help me pack up the food.'

Jimmy made a circle of his left index finger and thumb and jabbed his other index finger up and down inside the circle.

Hannah hoped that Juno had not seen this sickening gesture.

Jimmy jumped to his feet and said that he was not prepared to risk his horse by going any further. Those blankety-blank wheels on the konaki had to go.

Hannah was afraid. Without transport, she and Juno were in danger of becoming trapped here. They were entirely at Jimmy's mercy. His behaviour was becoming more disquieting by the minute. She did not believe the story about the dead lovers. The women in the settlement would have known about it and told the story over and over again. Stories of love and loss were their favourite tales especially when the characters broke the rules and were punished for it by an ever vigilant God.

Juno asked Hannah to read her tea leaves.

'Wait here,' said Jimmy. 'I need to go into the gully below and cut some totara.'

'What for?' asked Hannah.

'Makeshift runners for the konaki,' said Jimmy. 'We must get out of here.'

Hannah took Juno's empty mug and saw a tangle of dark brown tea leaves clinging to the sides. 'Bunches of grapes,' she said. 'Luscious fruit and an important journey.'

Juno smiled and clapped her hands.

Hannah could hear Jimmy thrashing about below them and then the rhythmic chopping of his axe. 'We have to go now,' she whispered. 'You fold the bed rolls and I'll pack the pikau.'

Juno pushed out her lower lip. This was her signal that she did not want to do what Hannah asked of her.

'We must leave here,' said Hannah.

Juno pushed her bottom lip out even further.

The sound of chopping stopped. Hannah, feeling more and more certain that they were in danger, told Juno that there were ghosts here, dangerous ones with little red eyes.

Juno sprang to her feet and folded up the bed rolls.

Hannah grabbed a water bottle and a canvas groundsheet from the konaki. She untied the horse's halter and smacked him lightly on the rump. Prince did not run away as she had planned. He stood there blinking at her in the morning light. She tried once more but again he just looked at her and blew air through his nostrils and stamped his white feathered feet up and down, up and down.

Hannah and Juno walked away as quietly as they could. Hannah turned for one last look at Prince and saw him toss his big head sideways, as if to say goodbye.

They struggled for hours through thick bush. Hannah had no idea where they were. She knew that they should try to find a creek and follow it downhill until it joined a larger river, but they seemed to be climbing uphill for most of the time. Although the rain had stopped the trees were still dripping with moisture. The bush was stirring with birds drying off their feathers. A few drowsy bees drifted around looking for nectar. The air smelled fresh and sharp with an aroma that Hannah recognised as rewarewa, the native honeysuckle. She took this early flowering to be a good omen that warm dry weather was on its way and that soon this wild wet winter would be over.

A kereru flapped noisily just above Juno's head. She shrieked and tripped over a fallen ponga. She shrieked even more loudly when she saw blood emerging from a rip in her woollen stocking.

Hannah tore the fabric away from the cut. She washed the wound with a handful of water from the bottle. She retrieved the package of sandwiches from the pikau and smeared her fingers with honey. She transferred the honey from her fingers to the patch of blood below Juno's knee. The blood thickened and the bleeding stopped.

Juno said that she wanted to go home. She hated the bush, she hated the bird that had tried to cut her legs off with its wings. If they had stayed with Jimmy he would have killed it stone dead.

'Hush now,' said Hannah. 'You must be brave. We still have a long way to go.'

Juno announced that she was hungry. Hannah waited until Juno had eaten some cheese and one of the thick pieces of bread before she suggested that they keep on walking.

Juno was reluctant to move. She said that her feet hurt and she was tired. Out came her lower lip again.

Hannah lifted her pikau onto her back. 'I'm off then,' she said. 'See you later.'

She left Juno lying against the fallen ponga trunk and did not look back. It was on the tip of her tongue to tell the girl that this journey was to save her from the clutches of strangers but she knew that it was pointless to try to make Juno understand her vulnerability. Juno had just one version of events, her own. Her world was what she saw from her own eyes and what she heard through her own ears.

Hannah remembered something that Sarah had once said; be careful not to build your life around another person. To love too much can be the worst sort of tyranny.

Juno's predicament was not the only reason Hannah was leaving the settlement. It had provided the catalyst and the justification for her actions but there were deeper issues at stake. The long period of solitude imposed upon her by the elders had given her time to think about herself. This was against the rules of the community. Selfishness, in all its manifestations, had to be ruthlessly stamped out.

Hannah heard something rustle in the undergrowth. She and Juno sometimes played hide and seek in the bush. It could be that Juno was creeping up on her. The undergrowth at the edge of the track was thick with the tangled spiked branches of juvenile matai.

Hannah left the track and crouched behind a tree trunk. She waited to hear Juno reciting the familiar chant, *coming ready or not!*

Something moved behind her. She jumped up and turned around. Facing her was a black and white dog, a border collie. The dog moved forwards slowly with its stomach close to the ground, stalking her. It did not take its eyes off her, she almost became mesmerised. She saw two eyes staring up at her, one brown the other a startling blue ringed in black.

'Here boy,' she said. 'Here boy, come here.'

The dog seemed confused. It stopped in mid-track, lowered its eyes and trotted off without making a sound. Hannah wondered where the dog had come from. She knew all the dogs at the settlement. She had raised some of them from puppies, spoiling them until they were ready to be taken away by the men to be trained into working dogs.

This animal was out of its territory. Unless it was lost, there must be someone who had allowed it to come into the dense bush. The dog would know how to return to his master. Perhaps she could persuade the dog to come back to her and lead her down to cleared ground and to the river bank. She put her fingers in her mouth and whistled. Nothing. She whistled again, more loudly this time. Again, no response.

She was not looking forward to another night out in the high country with Juno. As if on cue, she heard Juno calling out to her. 'Where are you? Where are you?'

Hannah ran back along the track. She found Juno walking along slowly with her head down. Hannah said she was sorry for leaving her for so long. She asked her where the bed rolls were.

'Dunno,' said Juno.

'You must have left them somewhere. We can go back and find them together.'

'Jimmy took them.'

'Did you see him?'

'Dunno.'

'Never mind, it's not your fault. We can find some ferns to make a bed.'

Juno cheered up. 'Make a bed, make a bed.'

They walked on. Hannah told Juno about the strange dog with one brown eye and one blue eye. Juno claimed to have seen him too. He could not bark so he said hello chickadee to her instead.

Towards the end of the afternoon they stumbled upon a track that Hannah hoped would lead them out of the high country. Much to her relief, it did. They descended a steep hill. The bush thinned out. The ground beneath their feet became wet and swampy. Now, there were cabbage trees and rafts of dense green flax bushes and wading birds rising up into the fading sun.

They came upon a creek in flood. Hannah filled the empty water bottle. The light was deepening. They moved onto higher ground. Juno said she was hungry and tired and that there was a blister on her heel. Hannah said we will make a bivouac to shelter us for the night then we will eat.

She took a knife from her pikau and slashed some branches from a clump of silver ferns that grew close to an outcrop of rock. A cleft in the rock provided some shelter from the rising south-westerly wind. She unfolded the canvas groundsheet she had taken from Jimmy's konaki. Her initial idea was to string it up to make a roof but she did not have a cord to pass through the metal eyelets to secure it to the rock.

Juno played with a fern frond turning it round and round

from green to silver and back again. Hannah asked her to put it back on the ground with the others. It was part of their bed for the night. Juno refused. Hannah felt like shaking her but she knew that she must not show anger or fear in front of Juno. Every decision she made from this moment on would have a direct bearing on whether or not they survived.

'Don't wanna sleep here,' said Juno.

'But you like the silver leaves. Look how they shine.'

'I want to go to the little house.'

'We can't go back. Sarah would be angry with us.'

'Sarah not here.'

Hannah gave up trying to reason with Juno. She unwrapped the remains of the bread and the cheese wheel. Juno ate most of it and drank the water bottle dry. Then she announced that she wanted to go to the dunny to do number twos. Where was it?

'You'll have to use the ground,' said Hannah. 'Over there, well away from our shelter. I'll go back to the creek to get some more water. Stay close, don't stray.'

Juno nodded. Hannah made her way back to the flooded creek and refilled the bottle. She found a small bush of rangiora halfway up the bank and collected some of the leaves for Juno to use as toilet paper. She sat for a while on a flat rock looking down at the rushing water breaking over the sandstone outcrops at the edge of the bank.

The task of keeping Juno free from fear and physical harm was greatly magnified out here. Back at the settlement there were always others to share the burden. Perhaps she had been too hasty in stealing this needy and damaged child away. But things could be worse. This creek could lead them into a tributary of the Mokau. Tomorrow at first light she planned to follow the direction of the water to see where it takes them.

But first she needed to get both of them through the night.

She hurried back to their shelter. The wind had died down. The cabbage trees had transformed their spiked heads into stark silhouettes against the backdrop of a vivid sunset muddied by black streaks of dissipating rain clouds.

She reached the rocky outcrop. The canvas groundsheet and the pikau were gone. Where was Juno? She called to her. There was no reply. She called again, more loudly this time. Again, no answer. She put her fingers in her mouth and gave a piercing whistle. The rays of the dying sun slipped down another notch.

She sank down onto the fronds of silver fern and put her face in her hands. This was the end. Juno could be drowning nearby in a foul swamp, calling for her, deathly afraid. Or perhaps Jimmy had tracked them down and taken Juno away. This would explain the missing pikau and groundsheet.

Something touched her left leg. It was the dog with the odd eyes. He pressed his damp nose once more against her leg. He made no sound. Hannah grasped his collar. She was determined that the dog was not going to leave her again. She tied her headscarf onto his collar to make a short lead. The dog did not seem to mind and made no effort to get away. She walked him around the rocky outcrop for a few minutes. She had hoped that he would take her to Juno. 'Seek,' she said. 'Seek, seek.'

But he just stared up at her with one luminous blue eye and one dull brown one, docile, obedient, walking when she walked, stopping when she stopped.

Then she saw it; a light shining from within a dense cluster of manuka and cabbage trees in the distance.

She ran, holding onto the short lead on the dog's collar, almost choking him in the process.

The light had seemed close at first but the more she ran, the further away the grove of trees seemed to be. Her shoes were heavy with mud and her calf muscles were stricken with cramps. A tremor began to beat inside her chest; tick tick tick. She wondered if she was losing her senses.

Then the dog stopped running. He lay flat on the ground and rested his face on his front paws. Hannah untied the headscarf from the dog's collar. 'Sorry boy,' she said. 'You are as lost as I am.'

The dog jumped to his feet and set off at a good pace. He ran ahead of Hannah and when she faltered he waited for her to catch up. Ah, there were the cabbage trees and the manuka and there was the light, stronger now. She did not see the hut at first. It blended in perfectly with the trees that sheltered it. It was a raupo hut, partly demolished, but with most of the walls still intact. And yes, there was a fire burning inside. Wisps of smoke threaded between the gaps in the bundles of nikau palms that formed the low-slung roof. A finger of smoke rose from the slab chimney set apart from the back wall. The entrance lay open to the weather, the door long gone.

Juno was inside, sitting on a wooden butter box close to the chimney, holding her hands out to the fire. Hannah restrained herself from reprimanding her. The main thing was that her sister was safe.

The hut was old and did not seem to be inhabited. There was a rectangular gap in the side wall that could have performed the function of a window but there was no glass, just the chewed remnants of a sheet of unbleached calico that someone had tacked over the opening to keep out the wind.

'Rats,' said Juno. 'Eat everything.'

There was a pile of dry bark and some small logs stacked neatly near the chimney. The pikau and the canvas groundsheet were placed upon the clay floor.

'Do you like our little house?' asked Juno.

'It's lovely,' said Hannah. 'You are very clever. How did you light the fire?'

'I took the Swan box from your pikau.'

'You should have waited for me. That was our last match.'

Juno pushed out her lower lip. To distract her, Hannah drew her attention to the dog lying down at the doorway. Juno patted him and tried to make him enter the hut but he would not. Hannah said that is yet another proof that he is a working dog, trained to stay outside.

'Someone must be out looking for him and that comforts me.'

Juno smiled. 'Look, on the shelf.'

'Food tins?'

'I put one on the fire. Dunno what's inside, rat got the label.'

Hannah grabbed two pieces of wood to use as a lever to pluck the tin from the flames. The tin was already bulging. Juno laughed. Hannah waited until the tin was cool and then stabbed it with her knife. A putrid smell of dead fish blew out into their expectant faces.

After her initial shock, Juno laughed again. Then she pleaded for something nice to eat. She claimed that her stomach was like an empty paper bag with teeth and that it had started to eat itself.

Hannah took a flannel from the pikau and moistened a corner with a little water. She wiped Juno's face and hands. She explained that there was just half a piece of bread left. It must not be eaten tonight. They would share it in the morning.

Juno yawned. She said that she could not stay awake. Hannah made a nest for her out of the canvas groundsheet. The dirt floor in the centre of the hut was hard and shiny unlike the damp sections at the sides of the hut. But Juno did not want to go to sleep in the middle of the floor. She said that things can walk around her and when the fire goes out it will be too dark to see the old people standing at the end of her bed. Hannah promised that she would try to keep the fire burning all night. Juno grumbled a little longer but soon her eyes closed and she fell into a deep sleep.

Hannah slept fitfully throughout the long night. She was vaguely aware of a passing storm that dumped a copious amount of rain on their shelter. She was surprised at how dry the floor was in spite of the open doorway and the holes in the roof. Once she heard something or someone howling mournfully through the trees. This thing seemed to call her name but in the end she decided that it was just the wind. She awoke stiff and cold and hungry. The fire had almost died down. She fed the embers with some dried bark and some of the smaller pieces of wood. Soon, small red and yellow flames licked around the edges of the logs. She held out her hands to the warmth and felt a flicker of life move up into her arms.

She hobbled outside the raupo hut to find a place where she could pass water without disturbing the still sleeping Juno. The wind had died down taking the rain with it. The dawn light filtered through a thin mist that shrouded the tops of the cabbage trees. The silence hummed. She crouched underneath a clump of manuka. The hot urine splashed against the inside of her thighs.

The smoke from the fire drifted slowly upwards from the top of the slab chimney. There was no sign of the blue-eyed dog. Hannah wiped herself with her headscarf. She wondered what Sarah would think if she could see her doing this. She tied the damp cloth to the manuka as a token of her presence here, or perhaps to leave a message.

She did not know what to do. She did not want to spend another day walking. Both she and Juno needed to rest. They had little food left and after the experience with the rotten fish the night before she was not pinning her hopes on finding anything edible in the remaining tins.

She went back into the hut and put some more wood on the fire. Juno awoke and began asking for food. Hannah told her that she thought it best that they stay here for one more day and one more night so that they could rest. Then they would follow the river to find some houses and people who would feed them. Juno said that she wanted to leave right now. She had liked the little house yesterday but not today.

Hannah opened her pikau to retrieve the last piece of bread. All that was left was a chewed piece of brown paper and some fresh rodent droppings.

'The rats, the rats, the rats,' said Juno.

'I forgot all about them.'

'I want my breakfast.'

'You win,' said Hannah. 'Let's go.'

They walked for hours along the river bank. The water was high and brown and agitated. Sometimes, they had to clamber up crumbling chalk banks and sandstone rocks in narrow canyons to keep themselves from being swept away by the floodwaters. Juno kept up a low grizzle of complaint. Hannah tried to make their journey into a game but Juno refused to participate. Hannah made sure that they stopped often to rest their feet. Each time they set off again Juno asked the same questions. How much longer? Where are the houses and the people?

In the late afternoon the rain came back. The icy needles pierced their naked faces. They were soaked through, hungry, tired, and lost. Juno's hands were blue. Her eyes had retreated into their sockets. She had stopped complaining and this worried Hannah far more than the incessant questions. Juno was tiny for her age, frail, and with soft bones. She was not able to cope with the ordinary vicissitudes of life. This had been told to Hannah often enough by Sarah and Augusta. Hannah had resisted this view of Juno but now, watching her body shut down, she knew that they were right.

Hannah decided to leave the river bank and find some trees or overhanging rocks where they could get out of the rain. They struggled up the river bank and shortly came upon a clump of regenerating manuka. Hannah spread the canvas sheet on some low branches and they crawled beneath it. She took a small towel from her pikau to rub down Juno's face and hair but it was soaking wet. All of their things were.

Juno fell asleep almost at once. Hannah tried to rouse her but could not. She was becoming afraid. Was this the place where death would come to take Juno away from her? She was no longer concerned with her own survival. Apart from her blistered feet and her swollen ankles she felt strong enough to walk out of this place and find a settlement on the river even if it took several days.

Night fell. Hannah drifted into sleep. The first thing she knew about the return of the odd-eyed dog was his hot tongue licking her cold wet face. She clung to his fur and pleaded with him not to leave her. The dog obliged. Although his coat was wet his body was warm. Hannah pushed him close to Juno. She stirred and put her thin arms around his neck. They huddled together beneath the canvas sheet for what seemed to Hannah to be an interminable length of time.

Towards dawn, she heard a muffled whistle coming from the distance. The dog pricked up his ears. Hannah was instantly on the alert. Was it Jimmy coming to find them? The whistle came again, much closer this time. Hannah heard a horse whinny. The dog jumped to his feet. Hannah tried to hold on to him but he was too strong for her.

Hannah crawled out from the canvas cover and walked a short distance to the edge of the regenerating manuka. If it was Jimmy who had found them she knew that she had to seek help from him. She had no choice. Juno must survive.

But it was not Jimmy, it was Mr Cattermole, leading two horses roped together.

Hannah took him to the canvas shelter.

'Jesus wept,' said Mr Cattermole.

He wrapped Juno in a grey wool blanket and placed her on the pack horse.

Hannah was relieved to see packages of flour and other supplies in the bottom of the saddle bag.

'Come now,' said Mr Cattermole. 'We must return to the raupo hut.'

'Is there not somewhere closer?'

'It's only about a mile from here.'

'But we walked for hours.'

He smiled. 'You went round and round in circles.'

'But we followed the river.'

'It snakes back on itself, a tricky beast that has led many men astray.'

Hannah stumbled. Mr Cattermole offered to lift her into the saddle of his lead horse. She declined. She wanted to stay on the ground, putting one foot down after another, her mind grappling with the possibility that Mr Cattermole could be a threat to her and Juno. He was a stranger after all, and someone from outside. The category of outsider was one that she had learned to fear since she was five years old. She could not forget that Mr Cattermole had winked at her during the community hearing, a wink that seemed to say *only we know what really happened when you clamped your ruby lips to mine...*

She had many questions to ask him. Had he been following them? Had he sent the dog as a messenger? How did he know that she and Juno had sought shelter in the raupo hut?

He extracted a tin from the inside pocket of his oilskin coat and with great ceremony offered her a barley sugar. A warm rush of sweet saliva filled her mouth.

'That tasted even better than the balm of Gilead judging by the look on your face,' said Mr Cattermole.

Juno stirred and opened her eyes. She thought it a great joke to be riding on the back of a pack horse. Hannah was so relieved to hear her giggle that she almost forgave Mr Cattermole for making fun of a sacred text. She was even more relieved when Juno noisily crunched two sweets at once and smiled through her dribble.

Soon, the raupo hut came into view. Mr Cattermole tethered his horses to a ponga hitching post near the entrance. Hannah could not remember seeing it there before. It looked freshly cut. The axe had bitten off the top of a young fern and cut the trunk into three lengths releasing a tangle of fine brown fibre.

The dog lay down across the entrance to the hut staring at Juno. Mr Cattermole told her not to be offended. 'Jacka's an eye dog, he's been trained to sit very still and give sheep the evil eye.'

'Baa baa,' said Juno.

'Jacka kept us warm through the night,' said Hannah. 'He probably saved our lives.'

'No,' said Mr Cattermole. 'This did.'

He removed a headscarf from the front pocket of his oilskins. 'Jacka brought it to me. You wore it during the trial, so I knew that it belonged to you. I gave Jacka the command. Find boy, find and stay . . . and he did.'

Hannah prayed that the rain had washed the smell of her urine from the scarf. 'Let's unpack the food now,' she said. 'Juno is very hungry.'

Mr Cattermole laid out a feast on a sheet of newspaper; a piece of cold damper, a lump of yellow butter wrapped in cheese cloth, three thick slices of corned beef and a solitary hard-boiled duck's egg.

Juno asked for porridge.

'Eat what's in front of you,' said Hannah. 'Please.'

'I need to make the fireplace safe before we can cook,' said Mr Cattermole. 'It's a wonder you didn't set fire to the chimney the state that it's in.'

Juno cracked the duck's egg on the back of her head. It took several blows for the pale blue shell to shatter. Juno took a bite and immediately spat it out.

'Has it gone bad?' asked Hannah.

'Baby inside,' said Juno.

She shed a tear for the tiny bird all curled up within the blooded yolk. Hannah consoled her by telling her that when they had found a safe place to live, Juno could keep some chickens and perhaps a pet duck if there was a creek or a pond nearby.

Juno devoured the butter that was wrapped in the cheese cloth.

Hannah did not have the heart to reprimand her for being greedy. Anything that diverted her from the tiny embryo was welcome.

After breakfast, Mr Cattermole announced that they would be staying in the raupo hut until the weather had improved and the horses were rested. There would be plenty of hot food once he got the fireplace and the slab chimney into a workable condition. There were other repairs to be done too; the hut needed a new roof, the floor needed to be re-sealed with wet clay, and there were essential furnishings that were once here but had been stolen away. 'And here's the grand thing ladies, everything we need to refurbish our mansion is growing outside and waiting to be plucked without spending a single penny.'

Hannah asked him if the hut belonged to him. He told her that no one owned it. It had been there for many years. Some locals say that it goes back to the days of the land wars and is haunted by the ghost of a redcoat who died there.

Hannah did not like this talk of ghosts. Especially in front of Juno. She asked Mr Cattermole why he wished to make repairs on this place if it was not to be his home.

Mr Cattermole said that he and Jacka were occasionally hired to find lost sheep for a farmer. He used this place to rest up and cook a meal when he was on a job.

He lifted the sheet of newspaper from the dirt floor and began to tear it into strips. Hannah begged him to save it. She had always wanted to read a newspaper but she had never been permitted. Only the elders had this privilege.

Mr Cattermole handed it over. 'It won't be much use to you. Out of date.'

Hannah opened the page carefully and smoothed out the creases. At first she did not understand what it was that she was reading. The page consisted of classified advertisements looking for farm labourers, clerks, insurance salesmen, carpenters, handy men, bakers and drivers.

'So that's how it's done,' she said. 'You see a job in the newspaper and you go and get it.'

'It's not quite that easy,' said Mr Cattermole. 'You'd be better off looking in the women's magazines for domestic work and sewing, that sort of thing.'

But nothing could dampen Hannah's enthusiasm. The bottom half of the sheet carried illustrated advertisements for pills and nostrums that purported to cure everything from women's troubles to irregularity. Hannah particularly liked the look of Dr Beecham's Liver Pills; only 1/6 posted anywhere in the country and guaranteed to cure dyspepsia and the yellowing of the skin. Just the thing for Juno's delicate system.

Mr Cattermole gave Juno a nosebag of oats for the pack horse Ruby. He explained that this was an important job because the old mare was almost at the end of her life and could not forage as well as the younger lead horse.

Juno, full of smiles, carried the nosebag carefully out of the hut.

'Thank you,' said Hannah. 'It makes her feel part of things when she is entrusted.'

Mr Cattermole said that he had an ulterior motive. He did not want to upset the child with what he had to say. Did Hannah know that two people were out looking for them? He had chanced upon them, a man and a woman, and they had asked him if he had seen a woman and a girl travelling in a konaki driven by a young man called Jimmy.

'What did you tell them?' asked Hannah.

'Nothing. I had no idea at that stage you were out here getting yourself hopelessly lost.'

'They must be the people from the orphanage. They were coming to take Juno from me.'

'Why did you run away from Jimmy?'

'The wheels broke. I didn't want to wait. Jimmy had to cut new runners from the bush.'

Mr Cattermole began to say something about Jimmy but stopped when Juno came running back into the hut. She gave them the news that Ruby had eaten all the oats and had asked for more.

'Okay ladies,' said Mr Cattermole. 'Let's get cracking. Time for work now.'

Mr Cattermole made it clear that Hannah and Juno had to do more than just watch him. They would be expected to do some of the hands-on work. Their tasks would be replacing some of the leaky palms on the roof, gathering manuka sticks and mangemange for the construction of a bed, checking the raupo bundles that formed the walls of the hut and, most importantly, lining the fireplace with fresh turf.

Hannah made a fumbling attempt to cut fronds from a clump of juvenile nikau palms growing nearby. Mr Cattermole stepped in and showed her the correct technique with the machete. Soon she was hacking away, until he called out enough! There's only one roof to mend.

Then he suggested that she climb onto the roof of the hut while he handed up the palms and some long thin strips of supplejack. 'No chance of a light-weight like you crashing through the roof. It happened to me once. I almost broke my back.'

Hannah did her best to fasten the butts of the palm fronds to the ridge pole with the supplejack but she failed. Each time she tried to tie a knot, the supplejack sprang apart and left red welts on her hands and arms. In the end, Mr Cattermole removed his work boots and came up onto the roof to finish the job. He made it look so easy.

She wondered what Sarah and Augusta and the other women from the community would say if they could see her now; skirt hitched up, blood on her fingers from the sharp palm needles, rope burns from the tricky supplejack. Sarah believed that plants were just like people; they had souls and were capable of both good and evil. She said that supplejack is more menacing than most because it grows anti-clockwise in tangled circles and if you watch it very carefully you can actually see it grow inch by inch in a few short hours. Hannah recalled one of Sarah's stories.

Not too long ago and not too far from here, a woman lay deathly still in the bush for three days to hide away from the sorrows of the world. When they found her, she was trussed up like a turkey. The supplejack had wound around her neck; it had entered her mouth and lungs and pierced her already broken heart.

Hannah could not get enough of these tales when she was a child. It seemed to her that every dilemma had its resolution in one of Sarah's moral stories. Now, Hannah felt that she was in alien territory and that Sarah's voice was stilled, possibly for ever.

Juno was in ecstasy. Mr Cattermole had made her his builder's mate. It was her job to hand him the turfs lying in a neat pile on the floor. He told her how important her job was. One wrong move and everything could go up; oh he had seen it all including an idiot who stoked the fire with totara logs and it hissed and sparked and burnt the whole whare down with him and another shepherd in it. If not for Jacka breaking the door down and leaping all over him he would not be here today.

'Golden rule,' he said. 'Never trust a wooden chimney.'

He placed the turfs up the sides and the back of the chimney with the precision of a bricklayer. He took an iron bar that had fallen from the old fireplace and worked it into place. He hung two hooks from the iron bar, one for his blackened pot and one for his kettle. He poured a little water from a canvas water bag into the kettle and lit the fire with some sticks of white pine and the newspaper that had entranced Hannah.

In spite of Mr Cattermole's kindness towards her and Juno she remained wary of him. She found it difficult to read his behaviour. Back at the community the elders gave the orders and the women and younger men obeyed. She would never have been encouraged to repair a hut or use a machete. This was men's work.

The warning that Abraham had given her about becoming a bone-conjuror played constantly on her mind. He had more or less accused her of being one of those malignant beings who could bring back someone from the dead.

Mr Cattermole's drowned death mask haunted her dreams. The first indication that he was returning to life was a slight movement of his lips beneath hers. She found the memory of his wet mouth opening like a ripe fig beneath hers disturbing. She could switch this memory off while she was awake but her dreams were out of control. Sometimes the mouth opened out like a red sea anemone waiting closure by the flick of a finger, sometimes it became a foreign fruit that dissolved into a sweetness so intense that it jolted her awake.

Mr Cattermole said, 'a penny for them. Thoughts I mean.'

'Nothing,' said Hannah. 'I'm a little tired that's all.'

'Good.'

He prised the lid from the bubbling kettle with a stick and threw in a generous handful of tea. He waited until the tea had turned dark orange before he produced three chipped enamel mugs and a tin of condensed milk.

Hannah drank two cups of the hot sweet fluid. Juno had three. Mr Cattermole laughed. He said he had never seen such a greedy pair of girls.

The day wore on. Juno went to sleep on the canvas sheet on the floor.

'I can hear the wind turning towards the south,' said Mr Cattermole. 'We might be in for a rough night. I need you to come with me to carry the mangemange to make a bed.'

Hannah did not want to leave Juno alone. Mr Cattermole said he would instruct Jacka to stay at the door of the hut and guard her. Hannah reluctantly agreed.

It took almost an hour for them to gather the materials for the bed. When they returned, Jacka was exactly where they had left him and Juno was still fast asleep. Hannah relaxed. She helped Mr Cattermole to position the four forked manuka branches to make the frame of the bed. He tied two crosspieces into the forks, one at the head and one at the foot. Hannah laid pliable manuka sticks lengthwise and Mr Cattermole fastened each one onto the crosspieces. The final task was the laying of the mangemange to make a soft springy mattress. Once finished Hannah went outside and inhaled the fresh evening air. Her sister was safe, at least for tonight.

Juno awoke and insisted on being the first one to lie down on the new bed. She said that it was bosker even though it was only a pretend bed.

Mr Cattermole dropped a bundle of kindling close to the fireplace. 'No bouncing or you'll break it.'

Juno put out her lower lip. 'Jimmy let me.'

'Let you do what?'

'Jump in his bed.'

'Did he indeed.'

'I'm hungry,' said Juno. 'I want my tea.'

'Me too,' said Hannah, as she came back inside.

Mr Cattermole rummaged around in the saddle bag and

found three wrinkled kumara and two potatoes. When the fire died down he threw the potatoes and kumara into the ashes. Then he mixed up some flour and salt and water with his hands. The dough took on a greyish tinge. He prised open a tin and told Hannah to look inside and take a sniff.

'Pure pig fat,' he said. 'This is what makes my damper famous.' He mixed some of the soft white fat into the dough and kneaded it into a round loaf. He placed it in the iron pot and buried it in the hot ashes of the fire.

After a while, a comforting smell of cooking infused the hut. Juno asked if she could have the first slice of the bread. Mr Cattermole said that damper needed to cook slowly otherwise it would be raw in the middle. He poked the vegetables with the point of his hunting knife and pronounced that they were almost ready. He rubbed pig fat and salt over the skins and placed them onto an enamel plate.

Juno grabbed a hot potato and dropped it just as quickly. Hannah consoled her by kissing her hand. 'All better now,' said Juno.

Night fell. Mr Cattermole lit a tallow candle. It gave out a dim spluttering light and an unpleasant smell. He took the iron pot from the ashes and removed the lid with a stick. The damper was crisp and brown and delicious. They fell upon it like wolves. Mr Cattermole said the grit from the ashes added a little something to the taste.

Outside the hut the wind sang a lament, rising and falling in a minor key. Mr Cattermole said he had to see a man about a dog. He was away for what seemed to Hannah to be a long time. When he returned, Juno was lying asleep on the mangemange mattress and Hannah was sitting on the butter box close to the fire. Mr Cattermole said that it was good to see the little one recovering her strength. All she needed was fire, hot food, and a dry shelter.

Hannah sighed. 'You make it sound so simple.'

The heavy rain arrived suddenly. The hut shook and trembled like a wounded animal.

Hannah lay down beside the sleeping Juno and closed her eyes. She did not know if she was asleep or awake when she saw Mr Cattermole move away from the fire and climb into bed beside her.

She became acutely aware of his body pressing against her own. She made a resolution to stay awake until the dawn. It was not to be. Lulled by his even breathing and the rise and fall of his chest, she soon fell into a deep sleep.

This time she dreamed that she was the victim and Mr Cattermole the hero. It was her mouth rising and falling beneath his.

Sometime during the night the southerly died away and took the heavy rain with it.

Hannah awoke to the clatter of the iron kettle and the smell of hot oatmeal. The bed had moulded to her body during the night and she felt reluctant to move. Mr Cattermole asked if she had slept well. Hannah said yes and thanked him for his concern. Mr Cattermole said good old mangemange, no wonder they call it the bushman's friend.

They ate copious amounts of porridge and drank stewed billy tea in companionable silence. Hannah said that she would like to stay here until she and Juno had recovered their strength.

Mr Cattermole shook his head. 'We must keep on moving until we are in a place of safety.' He threw some clumps of turf onto the cooking fire to damp down the heat.

'Let's go,' he said. 'Time to move on.'

Chapter 2

At first, they made good progress. The terrain flattened out and soon there were signs of human habitation signposted by fallen trees and areas of burnt bush.

'At this rate,' said Mr Cattermole, 'we should arrive in the township at dusk.'

Hannah wanted to ask him why he was helping them and how he proposed to hide Juno from the officials at the orphanage. She tried to engage him in conversation but he mumbled something about little pitchers having big ears.

Three sheep with vacant eyes and heavy fleeces appeared from nowhere. The dog pricked up his ears. Mr Cattermole ordered Jacka to stay.

'The poor things,' said Hannah. 'They can barely walk.'

'They still belong to someone even though they are runaways.'

'Can't we help them?'

'Beware the farmer with his gun.'

'You mean we could get shot?'

'The dog could.'

Juno, who had slumped forward without speaking for most of the journey, heard this and lurched violently, almost falling off the horse and taking Hannah and the saddle with her. Mr Cattermole dropped the lead rope. He grasped Hannah's lower leg and released her foot from the leather stirrup.

Hannah tried to release her other foot but could not do so. Mr Cattermole offered to help her. He held her ankle a little too long for comfort; it was almost a caress.

Mr Cattermole checked the saddle by placing his hand between the girth and the horse's belly. He tightened it up and suggested to Hannah that she walk the rest of the way.

'I should not have allowed Juno to share the saddle with you,' he said.

'I'm happy to walk,' said Hannah.

'The worst is over. We'll soon be on a roadway.'

Mr Cattermole showed Juno how to put her hands into the gullet of the saddle and hold on tightly. Juno smiled for the first time since they had left the hut. She thought it great fun to be riding solo while Hannah plodded alongside her.

They arrived at a dirt roadway that twisted and turned through gentle slopes and sheltered valleys. The afternoon wore on. The hovering rain clouds that had threatened them in the morning had dissolved. There was a smell of warmth and growth to come. Hannah could almost hear the land stirring beneath her feet.

Occasionally they passed plain wooden farmhouses with smoke drifting lazily from lean-to roofs and once, an elaborate bay villa with ornate return verandas. The villa glistened white and pure at the end of a long metalled drive flanked by willows and elms. A regenerating stand of kahikatea stood guard behind the house. Plump sheep grazed in the side paddocks.

Hannah begged Mr Cattermole to stop so that she could rest her feet. Her shoes were giving her blisters and Juno was complaining of thirst.

'Very well,' said Mr Cattermole. 'We're making good progress.'

They travelled a little further until they came to a patch of thick native bush that came almost to the edge of the road. There was a sound of running water from behind the trees. Mr Cattermole lifted Juno from the saddle and placed his bed roll beneath a clump of tall ferns. 'Sit here and keep my dog company,' he said. 'That is your job.'

He led the horses along a track deeper into the bush and allowed them to drink from the creek. He refilled the canvas water bag at a higher point from where the horses drank and brought the water back to where Juno and Hannah waited.

Hannah offered to gather some twigs to make a fire for the billy. Mr Cattermole said that the wood was probably too wet to burn. 'Besides, someone may notice the fire and come to investigate. We need to be careful.'

All Hannah wanted at this moment was to go back to the white house. She had never seen a house like this before, either in real life or in a book. She closed her eyes and made a mental map of the place where they had watered the horses. The white house was just down the road in a southerly direction. She made a silent pledge to come back and visit the house, to see what sort of people could live in such a sanctuary. She was quite sure that she would be able to find it again.

'Come,' said Mr Cattermole. 'Time to hit the road.'

'How much longer?' asked Hannah.

'One more hour or near enough to it.'

Ruby the pack horse plodded along slowly at the back of the procession. Mr Cattermole had to reduce his walking speed to accommodate her. He said that she was an old bush pony who did not enjoy walking along a rutted dirt road. Although there were few cars in the district, there had been some unfortunate incidents with her taking fright when suddenly confronted with one of the noisy monsters.

Hannah did not want to confess that she too was a creature of the bush, even more so than Ruby. The horse had actually seen a car whereas Hannah had not. She knew that they existed but that was all.

All at once Ruby stopped walking. The lead horse felt the tension on the rope attached to his halter and also stopped. Jacka assumed a watchful position by freezing at the side of the road, one blue eye and one brown eye fixed on something ahead. Mr Cattermole cautioned Hannah to be silent by placing a finger to his lips.

Smoke billowed around the curve in the road. There was a clinking noise of shovels hitting gravel and of men laughing and talking.

Mr Cattermole grabbed Jacka's collar and walked him to the side of the lead horse. He told Juno to stay put.

He and Hannah turned the corner. 'There is nothing to be afraid of,' he said. 'It's just some workmen fixing the road but some of them might know me. Let me do the talking.' Hannah was shocked to see what she thought was a funeral pyre burning in the middle of the road. Logs of smouldering wood were laid in rows forming a rough platform. On the top of the platform were chunks of grey bricks.

One of the men threw down his shovel. 'Cattermole, you old bastard.'

'Thought it might be you,' said Mr Cattermole. 'How are you Clive?'

'Fit as a buck rat.'

'Didn't know you'd be making burnt papa this close to town.'

Clive tapped the side of his nose. 'Cheaper than metal, but don't tell the council that.'

The two men sat on a log that lay downwind from the smoke. Clive gave Mr Cattermole some tobacco and a packet of zigzag papers. Mr Cattermole rolled up a smoke, inhaled deeply, and announced it to be a breath of heaven.

Hannah stood awkwardly at the side of the road. There were two workmen tending to the fire. One was a young Māori. He tipped his hat at Hannah but she was too shy to speak to him. The other worker was a middle-aged white man with an unkempt beard and small pink eyes.

He came close to Hannah and smiled. 'How do Missy,' he said.

Hannah backed away. The old man smelled bad. She almost choked on the combination of unwashed clothes, rotting teeth and the acrid smoke coming from the makeshift kiln.

At last Mr Cattermole and Clive finished their smokes. They shook hands.

Mr Cattermole came back to Hannah. 'I spun Clive a yarn or two. We are safe now.'

They went back and retrieved Juno and the horses. They walked carefully past the burning pyre so that the horses would not be spooked.

Hannah endured a suggestive leer from the man who had called her Missy.

Juno wanted to know what those funny men were doing.

'Look down little one,' said Mr Cattermole. 'See how red the road is here? That is what the fire does. It turns grey brick into beautiful red papa for us to walk on.'

The sun slid down behind the trees. A cold wind sprang up and slapped their cheeks. Just as Hannah was becoming concerned about Juno's well being, Mr Cattermole announced that they had arrived.

Hannah peered through the gathering night. Was this Piopio? She saw a muddy dirt road and a row of buildings with flimsy wooden verandas.

Mr Cattermole tied the rope on the lead horse to a hitching post outside a shop. Hannah could see the flicker of a lamp behind the net curtains that covered the window. She peered within. She could just make out a male mannequin wearing a tweed jacket, white shirt, cream trousers and a blue tie.

Mr Cattermole gave Hannah her pikau from the saddle bag. He pointed out a sign above the door. *Chas. Cooper, Gentlemen's Outfitters (Established 1905.)*

'Knock at the door,' he said. 'Tell him I'm sorry that we've arrived late and I'll catch up with him tomorrow.'

'Can I knock too?' asked Juno.

'Of course,' said Mr Cattermole.

There was a sour smell of damp clay and horse droppings in the air. This, combined with the yellow lamplight illuminating the goods displayed in the window, triggered off childhood memories for Hannah.

She remembered the layout of the living quarters at the back of the shop. She remembered her tiny bedroom without windows where the scrim lining the walls flapped against the sarking during a high wind. She remembered the overgrown garden at the back of the shop full of towering scotch thistles and golden buttercups where once a great black bee had stung her on the mouth. She had cried out for her mother to come and rescue her but it was just another cry that was never answered.

Mr Cattermole rode off to find a night stable for the horses. She desperately wanted to go with him but her head was spinning, why had Mr Cattermole brought her to this house? Had it been his intention all along?

Juno knocked on the door. No answer. She banged on the door again. After a short delay the door opened and a woman stood there holding a candle. For a split second Hannah imagined that it was her mother but this fantasy vanished as soon as the woman opened her mouth.

'You're late,' the woman said in a low voice. 'Mr Cooper is not pleased. But come in anyway.' She opened a doorway at the back of the shop. 'Take note,' she said. 'You are forbidden to use this door again. There is private access at the back.'

They walked down a hallway that linked the shop to the living quarters. The parlour door was open and hot coals burnt in the grate. Mr Cooper was sitting in an overstuffed velour chair reading a newspaper. He folded the paper away and mumbled something beneath his breath that sounded almost like a curse.

There was an awkward silence. Hannah was afraid that Juno would say something out of place. She tried to catch her eye, to warn her, but Juno was staring at the fire. Before Hannah could stop her, Juno had grabbed a log of wood from the wicker basket at the side of the fireplace and thrown it into the fire. A shower of red hot embers fell out onto the hearth.

The woman admonished Juno by clicking her tongue against the roof of her mouth.

'Sorry,' said Hannah. 'She didn't mean any harm.'

'Cluck cluck cluck,' said Juno.

Mr Cooper asked the woman to fetch some food and drink for their guests. He waited until she had left the room before he invited Hannah and Juno to sit on the settle next to the fireplace.

He told them that Lena did not mean to be unkind. She was rather set in her ways and found children difficult to understand.

'Is she my mother?' asked Juno.

'Good lord no. Whatever gave you that idea?'

Lena returned with slices of brown bread and an enamel

jug filled with hot milk.

Hannah and Juno fell upon the bread and drank two cups each of the scalded milk.

Juno smacked her lips. 'More.'

'Say the magic word,' said Hannah.

'Please.'

Mr Cooper asked Lena to fetch something other than bread for the girls. Like that apple tart she had made for his dessert. Any left? Good, just the ticket.

Hannah, lulled by the warmth of the fire and the buttery taste of the pastry found it difficult to keep her eyes open. Juno too, had licked her fingers and declared herself to be as full as a tick and ready for a big sleep.

Soon, Lena led the way to the little windowless room at the side of the lean-to. The room was exactly as Hannah remembered it. Two narrow beds, two kapok pillows covered with striped ticking, two shabby eiderdowns almost bereft of feathers.

Hannah asked where her pikau was. Lena said she had no idea but if she cared to look beneath the pillows, she would find some nightshirts and a towel for their morning wash.

Lena left the room with strict instructions for Hannah not to relight the candle once she had extinguished it for the night. 'If a fire were to come, there is no way out.'

Juno fell asleep almost as soon as her head hit the pillow.

Hannah lost the feeling of warmth that had engulfed her in the parlour. She felt wide awake and in no mood to blow out the candle. It provided a welcome flicker of light against the background of the creaking scrim walls.

She had not been in this room since she was a small child. Something had happened to her here, something neither good nor bad, something too ephemeral to grasp. All she had was a fleeting vision of her mother's face leaning over her. Behind her, the hiss of a Tilley lamp and the smell of kerosene vapour.

A distant sound of a child sobbing. Then nothing.

When Hannah awoke, her bladder was full to bursting. She crept out of the windowless room and into the lean-to at the back of the building.

The long night appeared to be over. She opened the back door as quietly as she could. A watery sun shrouded in fog struggled to illuminate the denuded arms of fruit trees standing to attention in the long grass at the back of the property.

She walked quickly to the outhouse and relieved herself, thankful that it was too early in the day for the flies to be out and about. There was no lid on the wooden seat. She scooped up a measure of lime from the kerosene tin and threw it down the stinking hole.

Back inside the lean-to she rinsed her hands in cold water over the sink. Someone shuffled in behind her. It was Lena, wearing a bedraggled satin dressing gown and pink slippers decorated with silken pompoms.

Lena mumbled something about hot water. She led Hannah inside to the kitchen. The firebox in the range glowed with heat. Lena filled a kettle with hot water from the tap at the side of the range. She poured the water into an enamel basin and handed Hannah a sliver of soap.

'Where is your towel?'

'Still in my room.'

'Oh.'

'Shall I get it?'

'No, let Juno sleep.'

Hannah rubbed the soap into her frozen hands and soaked them in the hot water. Her fingers turned the colour of beetroot.

Lena removed the lid from a large iron saucepan at the back of the stove.

'Soaking,' she said. 'Can you cook oats?'

'Yes.'

'Bread? Scones? Mutton stew? Pork bones?'

'Yes.'

Lena stirred the oats and then sat down at the table. She took a tin of tobacco from the pocket of her dressing gown and rolled a smoke.

Hannah was surprised to see a woman smoking but said nothing.

'Well,' said Lena, 'if you've told the truth, you could easily get a job. How many did you cook for back in that place?'

'About twenty.'

'That's good.'

'Sarah and Augusta did most of it. I just helped.'

'And Juno? Is she able to work in a kitchen?'

Hannah hesitated.

'I get the picture,' said Lena. She stubbed out her cigarette and returned to the stove to stir the oatmeal. 'But take heart, you won't have to bear that burden for much longer.'

Hannah removed her scalded hands from the enamel bowl. She thanked Lena for providing the hot water. But now she must go to see to Juno's needs. She could become quite anxious in a strange place.

Lena laughed. 'You're your mother's daughter that's for sure.'

Hannah kept her voice light. 'Do you know Eleanor?'

Lena sat at the table facing Hannah and rolled another cigarette. 'If your father finds out I've even mentioned her name, I'm finished.'

'Just tell me one thing. Is my mother still alive?'

'Let's do an exchange. You want information from me and I want something from you.'

'I have nothing to give you.'

'I want to read your hand.'

Hannah asked her what she meant.

'I forget how ignorant you are,' said Lena. 'Mind you, it's not your fault that you were locked away from the world for years with a pack of god-forsaken loonies.'

It was difficult for Hannah to sit and listen to this woman mouthing falsehoods. She felt that she was betraying Sarah and the others by not challenging Lena's foul words about them.

But Hannah knew that Lena was a vital link to Eleanor. She had to keep the peace no matter what she said or did.

'Give me your left hand,' said Lena. 'But before we start, you must promise not to repeat anything that comes out of this reading. Especially to your father.'

Hannah nodded.

Lena said that she did not want to give Hannah the impression that she was just a housekeeper, she was somewhat more than that. Quite a bit more in fact, and if she had not been foolish in her youth and married a man who loved his beer more than her, well, she could at this very moment be Hannah's step-mother. Alas, that drunken pig would not give her a divorce. It almost broke Mr Cooper's heart that she was not free to marry.

Lena took hold of Hannah's left hand and turned it palm up. Hannah endured the probing of Lena's index finger.

'This is the heart line,' said Lena, 'the best place to start. Yours is immature but already there are clues to your essential nature, a bonus in one so young. It starts beneath the middle finger. This means that you are selfish in love. It explains your possessive attitude towards Juno. Look at the stress lines crossing the heart line. Again caused by Juno. Her situation is impossible. The sooner she is taken away to be delivered of the child the better. Then you will be free.'

'What child?'

Lena said something about men having one-track minds.

'This is impossible,' said Hannah. 'Juno would never let a man touch her.'

Lena said she must have. Unless her name is Mary and she has come back to earth to give birth to the next messiah. 'Look, jokes aside, I had no idea that you didn't know.'

Hannah stood up. Her legs were shaking.

Lena said that she was sorry to have to be the one to tell her about Juno. Hannah must discuss it with her father. 'Why do you think he paid good money to Wilfred to get you both out? But when you speak to your father don't tell him about the palmistry. He'll go off his head if he knows that I still dabble in it.'

Hannah fled the warmth of the kitchen for the chill windowless room where Juno lay sleeping. She looked flushed. Hannah touched Juno's forehead. It was damp.

She pulled back the eiderdown gently and touched Juno's abdomen. It was a little swollen. For a brief second she wondered if Lena was mistaken but then she felt an unmistakable flutter, a slight ripple ending in a decisive movement of a foot or a tiny hand.

So it was true then. This child, barely fourteen years old, had been forced to taste the sin of fornication.

Hannah had always known that she would never be free of her sister's needs but this unexpected complication plunged her into a state of despair. Juno could not look after herself let alone a baby.

Hannah uttered words of comfort to the sleeping Juno, words of forgiveness. The baby stirred within Juno's abdomen and Hannah imagined a faint ethereal whisper of thanks, a ruffle of sound like the dive of a kingfisher on a warm spring day into the river.

She imagined herself floating on her back with her plaited hair splayed out behind her in a net of glistening wet ropes.

Her river, her beloved place. Would she ever see it again?

In the early afternoon a brisk wind arose that melted away the remnants of the fog. A languid sun made a reluctant appearance from behind the clouds. Hannah was summoned to the parlour. Clouds of intermittent smoke blew out from the fire. Hannah sat stiffly to attention on the wooden settle trying not to choke on the fumes. Lena blamed the damp wood. Mr Cooper blamed blow-back caused by the unusual direction the wind was taking. First easterly then south-westerly. Why the devil can't it make up its mind? Reminds me of certain people who live in this blighted place.

The door to the hallway was bolted. This, according to Lena, was to keep Juno away. She had left her in the kitchen breaking down a lump of dough with the rolling pin. The child had to have some amusement.

Mr Cooper said they were not here for an idle chat. There were decisions to be made. He stared at Hannah. She dropped her eyes and clasped her hands tightly together.

There was a sound of heavy boots thumping along the hallway. The door handle moved. Lena jumped up and unbolted the door and Mr Cattermole entered, stamping his feet and rubbing his hands together. He went directly to the open fire and held his hands out to the smouldering logs.

There was a subtle shift in the room. The air lightened. The fire burned more cleanly. Mr Cattermole sat on the settle next to Hannah. His leg touched her left thigh encased in her long skirt. She prayed that he would not notice her change of colour.

Mr Cooper said that they were here to discuss Juno's condition. He was saddened and annoyed that Hannah had not been informed of it until this morning.

'Mr Cattermole said that he had thought it better to wait until they got back here in case Hannah spilled the beans to the women back at the community. Not that she would have done it deliberately, you understand.

Lena said that as far as she was concerned, no one outside the family knew and if they did, it was nothing to do with her. She was not a gossip. But she had felt duty bound to inform Hannah of the situation when she discovered that Wilfred had not. He should have told her the truth right from the beginning.

'Be silent woman,' said Mr Cooper. 'Wilfred almost lost his life in that damned river.'

'Hannah saved me with her breath.'

There was an awkward silence.

Mr Cooper knocked out his pipe into a glass ash tray. 'I'm coming around to the view that I should turn Juno in to the authorities.'

'Do you mean the people who run the orphanage?' asked Hannah.

'No, that was a smoke screen. Wilfred made up that story knowing it would weave its way through the community and silence any objection to Juno leaving.'

'Hold on Charlie,' said Mr Cattermole. 'I brought her here

in good faith. I thought that you were going to take responsibility for her.'

'Dr Graham is coming to the house tonight to assess her.'

'But he might put her into a mad house for life. Is this what you want?'

'I don't know what else to do..'

'Don't look at me,' said Lena. 'I feel sorry for the poor little soul but not enough to raise her baby.'

'Be quiet Lena,' said Mr Cooper. 'There's not going to be a baby. Not this one or any others. Dr Graham will make sure of that. He has modern ideas on such things.'

'You can't do this,' said Hannah.

Lena mumbled something about making tea and crept out of the room like a feral cat on the prowl but as she turned in the doorway, Hannah noticed a half-smile flicker across her face, a brief expression of triumph, a small victory won by the breaking of a rule about speaking her mind in front of her master.

Mr Cooper disturbed the fire with a poker. A shower of golden sparks flared out of the iron grate onto the hearth. His position was clear. Even though he had had little to do with Juno since she was born, he was not without compassion for her.

'However, she cannot give birth to this child and that's an end to it. And if I find the swine who took advantage of her, I'll break his jaw.'

'Not if I get to him first,' said Mr Cattermole.

Lena came back with a loaded tea tray. The cups and saucers and the milk jug were decorated with floral motifs. A plate of wine biscuits topped with sweet sultanas, a silver teapot and a china sugar bowl completed the ensemble.

Mr Cooper mentioned the lack of home-made fruit cake.

Surely their visitors deserved better than these shop-bought biscuits?

'Someone stole the last of the cake last night. Your long-lost daughter to be precise.'

Mr Cattermole risked a wink in Hannah's direction.

She remembered a similar conspiratorial gesture when Mr Cattermole had been brought in front of the elders but this time she was comforted by his attention. She wondered about the meaning of the fleeting sensual moments that had flared up between them on their journey to Piopio. She had no idea if he felt the same. Whether he did or not, it could not change the fact that she had allowed lustful thoughts to enter her body, and even more shameful, that she had enjoyed the sensation.

Stay calm, his winking eye seemed to say. We will find a way out.

The doctor did not arrive at eight as arranged. They waited in the parlour where Lena had poured sherry into a glass decanter and placed it on a tray on the sideboard alongside a bottle of single malt whiskey and a plate of sponge fingers.

Juno had helped her to make them. She was responsible for joining the two halves of sponge together with whipped cream. Lena told Hannah that she had made sure that the little one had scrubbed her hands before she allowed her into her kitchen. Poor child. But how could Hannah stand it? The repeating of certain words over and over again, the outbursts, the constant demand for attention.

Mr Cooper said that Lena and Hannah could sit in the parlour with him. He did not see the necessity of this at first, but Lena had insisted.

The clock on the mantelpiece chimed nine. Mr Cooper placed another log on the fire. Lena complained that the room was becoming overheated and that the cream was beginning to ooze out of the sponge fingers. Juno knocked on the door twice. Hannah had to return her to the windowless room at the back. The third time it happened, Mr Cooper, by now somewhat mellowed by generous nips of whiskey, suggested that Hannah stay with Juno until Dr Graham arrived. And please make sure that she is clean and tidy and ready for his inspection.

Juno was in a state. She rocked backwards and forwards making noises halfway between a groan and a sob. Her speech was jumbled and repetitive and would not have made sense to anyone else but Hannah. However, a communication of sorts passed between them and Hannah began to suspect that Juno knew more about what was happening to her body than she had otherwise thought.

Someone hammered on the back door. It was Dr Graham, fuming out loud about having to come to the back door like a thief in the night, with not even a lantern left burning to light his way.

Hannah overheard Lena apologising to Dr Graham. Mr Cooper had informed her that he left the front door of the shop ajar. She must have misheard him.

They moved down the hallway. The door to the parlour opened and there was a rumble of male voices and the clink of glasses. No one came to fetch her.

'Now Juno,' said Hannah. 'You must keep very quiet and do exactly what I tell you to do.'

Juno nodded. Hannah laid her down on the narrow bed and tucked her in. She closed the door quietly and crept down the long hallway. She could hear Dr Graham's voice clearly through the parlour door. He said that he had been tied up for hours with an old man with pneumonia. He was trying to die but his family would not let him go. Such a scene of resistance, it was like a Greek play. Yes another wee drop would go down well. Cursed fog is coming down again. Who'd be a country doctor?

Hannah had trouble hearing Mr Cooper's reply. He mumbled something about time moving on and the necessity for haste. She heard the settle creak and the shuffling of boots. She knocked on the door and Lena opened it.

'Come in,' said Mr Cooper. 'Graham, this is my daughter Hannah.'

'My God,' said the doctor. 'She is Eleanor reincarnated.'

'Can we move on?' asked Mr Cooper. 'Hannah, please fetch your sister.'

But when Hannah opened the bedroom door she saw that Juno had gone. She ran back to the parlour and told them what she had found.

Mr Cooper said damn and blast, then apologised for swearing in front of the ladies.

'Someone must have frightened her off,' said Lena.

'Ah ha! Very interesting,' said the doctor. 'She is behaving exactly to type.'

Lena said that she hoped that Hannah had not told the poor child what was about to happen to her.

Dr Graham held out his glass for another nip of whiskey. He had eaten two sponge fingers one after the other and his dark moustache was dusted with icing sugar. 'Mental defectives relate to stress like an animal. She will burrow down somewhere like a fox on the run.'

Something broke within Hannah. She tried to control it but it was too late. She began to sob. Tears ran down her cheeks.

Silence. No one attempted to comfort her. After a minute, Dr Graham consulted his pocket watch and announced that as far as he was concerned, his working day was over. He must go now and attend to the welfare of his horse.

Mr Cooper pleaded with him to wait a little longer. 'The situation is urgent. Soon it will be too late to intervene.'

'Thanks for the cakes Lena,' said Dr Graham. 'Delicious as always.'

Hannah managed to control her weeping. It helped to see how ridiculous the doctor looked with his whitened moustache imitating fake snow on a Christmas tree. If Juno were here she would come right out and say so.

Juno. Her unpredictable behaviour was always a problem but it belonged to her, it was a vital part of her. Hannah could not imagine any other state of being.

The doctor, a little unsteady on his feet from copious nips of whiskey took Hannah's hand in his and tried to bestow a kiss upon it.

Lena gasped. Hannah pulled her hand away.

'Steady on old boy,' said Mr Cooper. 'No need for that sort of thing.'

Lena marched Hannah out of the parlour and into the kitchen. She filled a basin with boiling water and threw in the supper plates. Hannah stood there with a tea towel in her hand watching Lena take out her anger on the kitchen utensils.

Lena expressed a wish that Hannah knew how to sort out the cutlery correctly. It was quite annoying to have to fish around in that dark drawer beneath the table when she was in the middle of cooking something.

Hannah asked Lena if she had offended her in some way.

'No,' said Lena. 'Not you.'

Hannah did not ask any further questions. She dried the dishes as carefully as she could and hung the tea towel neatly on the rack in front of the range. Lena sat at the table and rolled up a smoke.

Hannah looked out of the kitchen window and saw the fog wrapping a shroud around the trees and the outbuildings behind the shop. She decided to look for Juno there first. She could not bear the thought of Juno sleeping like a wild thing with only her night fears to keep her company.

'Come here and sit beside me,' said Lena.

Hannah reluctantly obeyed.

'I was against the baby at first,' said Lena, 'but after hearing Dr Graham carrying on I'm having second thoughts. I want to help you if I can.' She drew a mouthful of smoke down into her lungs.

Hannah had a sudden revelation. 'Maybe she's gone to find the horses.'

Lena exhaled then lowered her voice to a whisper. 'I know where they are.'

She stubbed out her cigarette and gave Hannah detailed instructions. 'Go out the back door and around the side of the house. Make your way to the street and turn right. Walk for about five minutes, briskly. You will end up at the bake house. There will be a yeasty smell of bread rising to guide you. Next to the bake house is a narrow right-of-way. Follow the corrugated iron fence to the back of the bake house. You will see a run-down building that houses a blacksmith. Wilfred Cattermole usually stables his horses there and sleeps in the bunk house provided for travellers.'

'I must find her,' said Hannah.

'You will need to wrap up warmly,' said Lena. 'Your pikau is in the washhouse.'

'Thank you,' said Hannah.

'Now that I have said my piece, I wash my hands of you. This conversation between us never happened. Understand?'

Hannah left the kitchen as quietly as she could. The door to the washhouse was stuck. The wooden door had swollen in the damp air. Hannah grasped the doorknob and pushed it with all her strength. It resisted her. She tried again and this time, the door opened. She froze. Someone inside the house must have heard the loud thump. She closed the door behind her and hid inside. Minutes passed. Her eyes became accustomed to the dim light. She saw her pikau hanging up near the wash tub.

She seized it with relief. Everything she owned was in this canvas bag. She opened the top flap and pulled out a knitted hat and a jumper. The wool provided instant warmth. She waited for another minute to pass before she felt safe enough to leave the washhouse.

She followed Lena's instructions by singing them softly to herself like an ancient navigational chant; follow the smell of hot bread, follow the corrugations of the dark tunnel, follow the sounds of horses snickering and stamping their hooves as the stranger approaches.

The fog made it difficult to find the tunnel but once she had discovered the entry to it, she ran her left index finger along the side to get her bearings. A memory came to her of running alongside iron fences as a child, holding a stick to the corrugations to make a *pitter pitter* noise. Perhaps it was this very same fence where she had made the music.

She turned a corner still hugging the iron wall. The courtyard was illuminated by a single lantern hung on the outside of a horse stall. She could hear Juno weeping before she saw her. The girl was lying down on the hay cradling the head of a fallen horse in her arms.

Mr Cattermole was leaning against the back wall of the stall. He saw Hannah approach and shook his head.

Juno raised her wet face to Hannah. 'Ruby won't talk to me.'

'How long has she been down?' asked Hannah.

'Not long,' said Mr Cattermole. 'But she won't be able to get up again. She's dog tucker and she knows it.' He wiped moisture from his eyes with a grubby rag.

Hannah crouched down and lifted Ruby's head from Juno's encircling arms. 'Leave her now. She's drifting away.'

The horse gave one last sigh and expired. Hannah helped Juno to her feet.

Mr Cattermole told Juno not to blame herself. If anyone had done anything to hasten Ruby's demise it was him. He had pushed a tired old horse beyond her limit.

Jacka appeared from nowhere. Mr Cattermole said that the dog had kept away while Ruby was dying. Pack instinct. But Jacka will miss Ruby as much as I will.

Mr Cattermole lifted Juno up into his arms and she put her wet cheek against his shoulder. They walked back towards Mr Cooper's shop. Hannah wanted to know how Juno had found her way to the stables. Mr Cattermole said that he had found her galloping along the road like a brumby on the run. She had fought him off at first but had soon calmed down.

They crept through the back door as quietly as they could. Mr Cattermole lit the candle stub. Hannah brushed and re-plaited Juno's long hair. Mr Cattermole tactfully turned his back so that the young girl could retain her modesty while Hannah helped her into her night attire.

He waited until the exhausted Juno fell asleep before he bid Hannah good night. He closed the door behind him leaving her with a guttering candle and an unspoken plea for help that she had been too afraid to initiate.

If her father had been able to provide them with the sanctuary that she craved, she and Juno could have stayed in his house and helped him in his work. But all he wanted was to obliterate the shame of Juno and what had happened to her.

For a brief moment she toyed with the idea of returning to the community; everything was structured there, predictable, safe. She dismissed this idea as soon as it entered her head. Conceiving a child outside marriage was considered to be a great sin. Juno would be severely punished.

Hot wax drowned the last flicker of candle light. Hannah drifted into an uneasy sleep and dreamed of breathing life into the body of a tiny child, who smiled at her revealing a perfect row of teeth and a quivering pink tongue; *only we know what really happened when you clamped your ruby lips to mine . . .*

The next day Hannah kept herself busy in the kitchen cleaning the iron pans and the dirty shelves. There was a layer of grey ash and mutton fat covering every surface. She scrubbed down the range with ammonia and brought it back to its original gleam with black polish administered with a small paint brush.

Hannah knew that it was only a matter of time before the doctor came to take Juno away. She must make a move as soon as possible even if Juno was still in a state of grief over the death of Ruby.

Juno slept until noon. Hannah hardly spoke a word to Lena. She made sure that she went back into the bedroom on the pretext of checking up on Juno when her father closed the shop and came into the dining room for his lunch.

Hannah helped Juno to dress. The child shivered. Hannah took off her jumper and wrapped it around her sister's tiny body.

'You must feed the little baby. It is hungry inside you,' said Hannah.

Juno stared at Hannah without blinking. Hannah found it unnerving to see those fixated eyes huge with unshed tears. It was like staring into a smoky mirror that gave no image back. Hannah had seen this look before. It had to do with Juno's inability to cope with the death of animals. Two incidents had profoundly affected her. Abraham had shot Juno's favourite dog because it had worried a sheep and Augusta had drowned a bag of unwanted kittens in the creek. Augusta had filled the canvas bag with stones to weigh it down and the baby cats had cried out in high mewling voices. Augusta did not realise, or so she later said, that Juno was hiding in the bush spying on her.

Several times after this event, Juno had crept up behind Augusta and mimicked the dying calls of the kittens. Augusta reprimanded Hannah for not controlling her sister's behaviour. 'Do something, or the Good Lord will guide my hand to make it stop.'

This was Augusta's signal that she was about to use the leather whip attached to the back of the kitchen door. This whip was especially made for children. It stung but did not cut too deeply into tender flesh.

Hannah instructed Juno to stop tormenting Augusta. All she got was the smoky mirror look. In desperation, Hannah told her that a feral cat had been seen coming out of the bush in answer to the distress calls. Perhaps she had rescued the kittens. Juno smiled and clapped her hands and the mewling ceased.

Lena came into the room. She ordered Hannah to come with her to the kitchen. She needed a hand with the cooking. There was to be a meeting here in the early evening.

'Don't ask me who it's with. Your father hasn't bothered to tell me.'

There was something in the tone of her voice that caused Hannah to wonder if Lena knew more about the meeting than she was prepared to disclose.

Lena asked what was wrong with Juno. Hannah said that Juno had a special relationship with animals and hated to see them suffer.

'So Wilfred's old mare finally kicked the bucket.'

Hannah was mystified. Lena seemed to know what was going on in this town without ever leaving the house.

Lena smiled. 'Jungle drums dear. Or to be correct, my precious party line.' Hannah had no idea what she was talking about.

Lena set up the mixing bowls and wooden spoons and baking trays on the kitchen table. She opened the drawer beneath the table top and complimented Hannah on the tidy placement of the kitchen implements within.

She placed some logs into the firebox of the range. She instructed Hannah to begin the cooking. The recipes were there in that folder. All handed down from her mother and her mother before her.

She sat at the table chain smoking and giving Hannah blow-by-blow instructions. Hannah did not need to read the recipes. She had been cooking since she was ten years old. When Lena instructed her to cream the butter and sugar before adding two beaten eggs to begin making a cake, she insisted that Hannah bring the bowl to her to be checked before she added the flour and the dried fruit. Once it was mixed to her satisfaction, she watched Hannah pour the mixture into a baking tin.

'Excellent,' she said. 'Now make the pastry for the apple tart. Rub ten lumps of butter the size of a walnut into three cups of flour. Deal with it quickly, a light touch is required. Your father likes his pastry short.'

Hannah did not tell Lena that she was already an expert. She deliberately made a few mistakes in the final recipe. Lena complained that the date scones were a little too flat. How much baking powder did she put in the mix? 'Use a little more next time and they will come out lighter. And did you remember to put two pinches of cayenne pepper into the cheese scones? Ah, I thought not.'

The day moved towards dusk. Hannah took Juno a cup of warm creamy milk and a slice of apple pie. To Hannah's relief Juno wolfed down the food then closed her eyes and fell into a deep sleep.

Lena called for her from the kitchen. Her face was flushed and she seemed to be in a good mood. She was drinking something brown out of a large china cup.

Mr Cooper came into the kitchen to see how the preparations were going. He inspected the plates of cakes and biscuits. 'Well done Lena,' he said. 'What a splendid spread.'

Lena sipped at her drink. 'Hannah helped a bit.'

'Glad to hear it.'

Lena asked what time the guests would be arriving. Mr Cooper consulted his pocket watch. He hesitated a little, then said, 'Hannah, I want you to get Juno prepared for a medical examination. Dr Graham is arriving before the others for this purpose.'

'But she's sleeping and should not be woken.'

'This whole business is a nightmare,' he said. 'But I'm not blaming you for anything that Juno did.'

'The child is lucky to have a sister like Hannah,' said Lena. 'She reminds me of Eleanor.'

'Enough!' Mr Cooper hit the table with a closed fist. 'Hannah, come with me. I'm sorry that you had to hear this.'

Hannah desperately wanted to stay in the kitchen and ask Lena about Eleanor. But her father took her arm and propelled her firmly down the hall and into the parlour.

He sat in his usual chair and filled his pipe with tobacco and tamped it down. 'It's the drink talking, not her.'

Hannah knew very little about alcohol. The men in the community made beer from fermented barley but the women were not permitted to drink it.

Mr Cooper said that he was grateful to Hannah for caring for Juno but the time had come when he had to take control of the situation. The baby must be taken away from her.

Hannah said that she was more than willing to care for the child.

Her father frowned. 'Maybe I am not making myself clear. Juno is mentally defective. There are laws being drafted that will make sure that girls like her do not breed. The men that are coming here tonight are part of a group involved in the eugenics movement. This committee has strong ideas surrounding mental defectives. They are a danger to the purity of our race. They must be sterilised and contained. The committee has done me the honour of making me the president of their newly-formed society.'

Hannah managed to control her voice. 'What do you want me to do?'

Mr Cooper looked relieved. 'This is a very delicate situation. Legally I mean. It will make it so much easier for all of us if you are on our side. Don't get me wrong. I am not without compassion for the girl but this is the best outcome for her as well as us.'

Hannah kept her silence. She did not trust herself to challenge him directly when it came to Juno's welfare. She was afraid that she might reveal her intention to leave Piopio with Juno in tow as soon as possible.

Mr Cooper said, 'Now run along my dear and sit with Juno until the doctor comes.'

She went back to the kitchen. Lena was slumped over the table. Hannah shook her awake.

Lena opened one bleary eye. 'Oh it's you again,' she said.

'You must tell me where my mother is. They are going to hurt Juno.'

Lena sat up and opened both eyes. 'Don't be ridiculous.'

Hannah felt the panic rising up into her throat. 'But my father said . . .'

'Juno will be fine. They will give her some medicine and she won't feel a thing.'

'Will the baby die?'

The doorbell at the front of the shop rang.

'Go quickly Hannah,' said Lena. 'I will delay the doctor as long as possible. Slip out the back door. Find Wilfred.'

But it was too late. The kitchen door opened and Mr Cooper and Dr Graham came in.

The fresh baking was laid out on a fancy platter on the side board. Next to the cakes was a batch of scones covered over with a linen tea towel. The doctor asked if he could take one. Lena said help yourself.

Mr Cooper said, 'I don't want to hurry you Graham but I think that you should do the deed before the others get here.'

'Of course,' replied the doctor, his mouth full of warm cheddar and melting butter.

Mr Cooper looked uneasy. 'Do you need me?' he asked.

The doctor took a snowy white handkerchief from his breast pocket and shook out the folds. He wiped his face and moustache with a ritualistic movement; wipe flick wipe flick. He asked for a bowl of warm water and a hand towel.

'Your presence is not required. However, I will need either Lena or Hannah to help me restrain the child on the table.'

Lena refused point blank.

They all looked at Hannah. She agreed to help him. But there were certain conditions. Juno must not feel any pain. Did Dr Graham have access to chloroform? And the room without windows was too cold and dark to be safe. They would have to move to the parlour where the light was good and the fire crackling with warmth. A clean sheet was required to cover the dining table. Also, some clean towels to place between Juno's legs if she began to bleed.

Mr Cooper asked Hannah if she was a nurse. How else would she know these things? Hannah did not bother to inform him about her work as a healer during the flu epidemic. She was focussing on her plan of escape. The room with no windows was a dead end in more ways than one. The move to the parlour would make it easier for her to get away. But she needed help. It had to be Lena. There was no one else.

Mr Cooper looked at his pocket watch. He frowned and said time is marching on. The others will be here soon.

The two men left the room.

Hannah waited until she heard the parlour door close before she whispered to Lena, please help us, please.

Lena said Hannah should ask Wilfred, not her, there was nothing she could do now. Mr Cooper would put her out on the street if he thought that she was being disloyal to him.

For a fraction of a second Hannah lost her focus. But then she heard Juno running along the hall calling out to her. She opened the kitchen door and Juno flung herself into her arms sobbing and tFLena selling an incoherent story. Something about waking up and seeing all the old people standing at the end of her bed chanting, get out get out.

Hannah held onto Juno's arms. 'Stop,' she said. 'Stop this silly nonsense at once.'

And Juno did. She was clearly shocked at the tone of Hannah's voice.

Hannah held onto the child with all her strength. 'Now listen. We are going to play a game and you must promise me that you will do everything I tell you.'

'I promise,' said Juno.

'Even if you get frightened?'

'I promise.'

Lena said that she was sorry for not supporting Hannah and was there anything she could do?

Hannah did not bother to answer her. She took Juno's hand and went into the parlour. Her father had a cheerful blaze going in the fireplace and the doctor had already set up a make-shift examination couch by covering the table with a sheet as requested.

Hannah said, 'This is the beginning of the game Juno. This is a pretend bed and you have to lie on it just for a little time and close your eyes.'

Mr Cooper said with forced cheerfulness that it was time for him to leave. He closed the door behind him with a soft click.

The doctor praised Hannah for her treatment of Juno. 'Quite remarkable,' he said. 'She is putty in your hands.'

Hannah undressed Juno down to her underwear, leaving her camisole and her pink bloomers intact. Juno lay with her eyelids shut, quivering a little, but submitting with grace. Hannah saw that Juno's legs had become thinner than ever. There was not an ounce of fat on her stricken body. Her pregnancy was beginning to show. There was something ludicrous about the possibility of a living child taking refuge undergo a hysterectomy as soon as possible after the birth. The hospital at Taumarunui would be the best place for her to go. There was nothing suitable in this district.

Juno asked if the game was over now.

'Yes,' said Hannah. 'It wasn't too bad was it?'

Juno opened her eyes. She liked it she said, it's a good game. She'd done it before. Jimmy had taught her. He pushed something into her and it hurt and he made the hurt go away by rubbing her in a special place. And she liked it. Was the doctor going to do it?

Dr Graham poured himself a large whiskey and gulped it down. He asked Hannah to make sure that Juno did not speak to anyone about what had happened to her. Nobody would believe her. Who is this Jimmy anyway?

Hannah dressed Juno and left the doctor to his whiskey.

They went back into the kitchen. Juno, cheerful now, ate two pieces of ginger crunch and a date scone.

Lena said it's a miracle, a miracle. She kept touching Juno's hair.

Hannah could barely breathe. She had never felt hatred like this before, hatred for Jimmy and for everyone who had aided and abetted his crime. It was becoming increasingly clear to her that Sarah must have known. Otherwise, why had she helped her and Juno to escape? Who could she trust? Now that Juno had named her tormentor, the doctor would surely pass it on to her father and Mr Cattermole. Lena had been her only ally and even then, she gave conflicting information.

'Leave her hair alone,' said Hannah. 'She does not like being touched.'

Lena's face crumpled. 'Sorry.'

Hannah regretted speaking harshly to Lena. She had been kind to her and Juno, or at least as far as her relationship with within such frailty.

Hannah said, 'Now Juno, we are going to play the next part of the game. We are going to talk to the little baby and to do this, we need to go inside your stomach.'

'Da da da,' said Juno.

Hannah asked him for the chloroform bottle in case Jun panicked. Did he have a Skinner mask? Good. In the black ba

The doctor nodded. Quick as a flash Hannah placed h hand within the bag and seized a bottle and a folded cott mask. She slipped them into the front pocket of her smo

The doctor put on a rubber finger stall and lubricated it v Vaseline. He pulled down Juno's bloomers and inserted finger into her vagina. He palpated her abdomen with other hand.

Hannah held her breath. Juno kept her eyes shut and one note that seemed to last for ever, high and fresh and

'Keep singing little bird,' said Hannah.

The doctor frowned. He removed the finger stall and Juno's bloomers up.

The doctor was leaning on the mantelpiece. H advanced so quietly that he did not notice her. Bu without turning to face her he told her that unfort the operation was off. She's too far gone. At least fiv months.

Hannah was shocked but relieved. Her plan to re doctor unconscious with the chloroform had little c success from the outset but she could not think of else to do.

The doctor berated her for not noticing the p sooner. Hannah apologised. She asked him what wou to Juno now.

He said that she would have to go full term. An

Mr Cooper allowed her to be.

'Forgive me,' said Hannah. 'I'm the one who should be sorry.'

Lena rolled up a cigarette. She twisted a piece of newsprint and attempted to light it from the hot wood ash in the firebox.

'There are some matches left in the candle holder in the back room,' said Hannah.

'Come too?' asked Juno.

Hannah shook her head. She needed to find a secure hiding place for the two objects hidden in the front pocket of her smock. It was only a matter of time before the doctor discovered her theft. She suffered a small twinge of guilt but quickly suppressed it.

She entered the room without windows as quietly as possible. She found a small hole in her kapok mattress and tore it open. She placed the bottle of chloroform and the folded mask inside and replaced the grey blanket over the ticking. She got to the door of the bedroom before she remembered the matches for Lena. There were just four left.

She could not bear to think of what could happen to Juno if she was taken to Taumarunui Hospital to have her child stolen away and her womb removed. That would be the end of Juno's fragile grip on reality. She would cross the line into madness, locked away, weeping, wailing, calling for her.

Hannah was relieved that she had a weapon of sorts. A few secret drops of chloroform could render the strongest man unconscious.

She heard the scuffle of leather shoes on the hall floor and low male laughter and the clink of whiskey glasses.

The committee had arrived.

The last two hours Hannah spent in her father's house were exhausting. Lena, primed up with constant sips of beer, kept up a running commentary on snippets of conversation that she overheard while re-filling the whiskey glasses.

Hannah begged Lena to stop. It reminded her of the council of elders back at the community when they were making their judgments against her. Now Juno was in the firing line, the victim of a group of men who were hell bent on destroying her. It was almost as if they were afraid of her. But why? Juno was a child of nature. She could not grasp the notion that anyone would act with malice or ill intent towards her.

Hannah posed this question to Lena. She was of little help. All she knew was that they were plotting to medically mutilate the poor child and that was wrong.

Hannah and Juno pretended to go to bed. Lena, slurring her words a little, gave Juno a hug and told her to be good. Hannah thanked Lena for her help. She was surprised to see Lena's eyes fill with tears.

Lena said that she would miss them both. Whatever little she had done for them was because of her debt to Eleanor, no, she can't talk about it. Maybe one day, when she is finally free of this place.

Hannah waited until she heard her father's bedroom door close. Then as quietly as possible she woke Juno and whispered in her ear, time to go little one. Juno, who seemed to sense the gravity of the situation, obeyed every instruction that Hannah gave her. They went out the back door and crept along the road to the stables where Mr Cattermole was waiting for them with Captain saddled up and ready to leave.

'Thank you,' said Hannah. 'I wasn't sure if you would be here.'

'Lena persuaded me, she told me about what happened to Juno.'

Juno asked to see Ruby one last time. She pushed out her lower lip when Mr Cattermole said she was too late. The cart had come to take her away. Ruby was in horse heaven.

He put Juno on Captain's back. The night enclosed them in a thick yellow fog. Mr Cattermole claimed that this sort of weather was ideal when stealing away from the coven of busy bodies and curtain twitchers who lived in this blighted town. The water vapour in the air muffled the clip clop sound of departing hooves.

Captain stopped on the outskirts of the town and looked behind him.

'He's looking for Ruby,' said Mr Cattermole.

'Do horses feel sad?' asked Juno.

'Of course.'

Juno wanted to know where Jacka was. She said that she missed his blue eye.

'He'll turn up when he's good and ready,' said Mr Cattermole.

The road twisted and turned. The fog began to thin out. Hannah asked Mr Cattermole where they were headed. He grunted something she did not quite catch.

She had a strong sense that she had travelled this road before but in reverse. This became a certainty when they saw a platform of half-burned logs on the side of the road. It was the place where they had come upon workmen making burnt papa. Some grey bricks were scattered behind the logs. A shovel and a hatchet lay on the ground.

'What a shame that the workmen were so careless,' said Mr Cattermole, picking up the tools. 'These will come in handy.'

'But they don't belong to you,' said Hannah.

Mr Cattermole laughed. 'Finders keepers losers weepers.'

They travelled on until the fog melted away to reveal a faint tinge of pink in the eastern sky. Juno, riding high in the saddle, claimed that she could hear a faint bark. She insisted that Jacka was near. And that he was crying.

Mr Cattermole gave a piercing whistle. Nothing. He did it again. Still nothing.

'A false alarm,' said Mr Cattermole. 'Let's move on before our escape is revealed.'

But Juno insisted that she could hear the dog. She swung her leg awkwardly over the saddle and fell to the ground. The burnt papa had built up a thick layer of fine gravel at the side of the road and this, to some extent, cushioned her fall.

Hannah picked her up and comforted her as best she could. She was angry with herself. She should never have allowed her sister to ride Captain in her condition. What if the baby had been injured and Juno suffered a miscarriage?

Mr Cattermole did not seem too worried about Juno's fall. He said for the life of him he could not understand why the two girls had never been allowed to learn to ride. He had fallen off dozens of times when he was a young lad. Never did him any harm.

There was a disturbance in the scrub at the side of the road. Jacka appeared. The white fur around his neck was matted with biddy-bids and one of his back legs was covered in blood. Mr Cattermole said that it was unusual for an eye dog to bark. Thank goodness he exercised his vocal cords for once and that Juno had heard him.

Mr Cattermole tried to stretch out the damaged leg to see the extent of the wound but Jacka gave him a warning nip.

'He's been caught in a trap,' said Mr Cattermole.

'How did he break free?'

'God knows.'

Juno fondled Jacka's left ear and whispered something into it.

Hannah crouched down beside her. 'The wound needs stitching. It will not heal otherwise.'

Mr Cattermole frowned. 'We are a long way from a vet out here.'

Hannah offered her services. She had some basic medical supplies in her pikau. She had stitched up human wounds before and a dog would be almost the same.

'He would never keep still enough,' said Mr Cattermole.

Hannah took a fine-toothed comb from her jacket pocket and handed it to Juno. 'The biddy-bids must be removed. He will try to bite them out and this will cause him more pain.'

She showed Juno how to hold a clump of hair flat so that the comb would not pull on his skin. Jacka let Juno do it without complaint. He stared at her with his one blue eye open and his one brown shut as if mesmerised by her attentions.

Mr Cattermole sat down on a fallen tree trunk and rolled up a smoke. 'He's my mate. Maybe I should put him out of his misery.'

Juno's comb stopped in mid-air.

'No,' said Hannah. 'Let me try something else first.' She opened her pikau and took out the mask and the bottle of chloroform that she had stolen from Dr Graham's bag. She flipped the mask open.

'What the hell is that,' asked Mr Cattermole.

'It's a Skinner mask. I will place it over Jacka's mouth and nose and drop a small amount of chloroform onto it. He will go to sleep just long enough for me to clean out the wound and then sew it up.'

Mr Cattermole said that he was not convinced about using the chloroform. He had heard that sometimes things go wrong. Jacka might go to sleep and never wake up.

'Jacka is losing blood from his injured leg. We have to do something right now.'

'For Christ's sake be careful.'

Hannah took this as consent. She rummaged around in the saddle bag and found a small piece of canvas sheeting. She and Juno lifted the shivering dog onto the canvas. His head was sinking down onto his front paws and his eyes were beginning to glaze over.

'Quickly,' said Hannah. She gave the Skinner mask to Juno and told her to hold it just above Jacka's maw. 'Don't let it touch his face, he'll panic.'

Hannah held the chloroform bottle two inches above the thick gauze fabric that covered the wire frame. One, two, three drops. The dog gave a deep sigh and went to sleep.

'Take the mask away, but keep it close in case he wakes up too soon,' said Hannah.

Hannah washed out the wound with a little water. She dabbed iodine liberally onto Jacka's skin. It was difficult to stitch the wound without having a razor to remove the hair but the cut was deep and clean and she managed to sew the edges together with a fine needle threaded with black cotton. She asked Mr Cattermole to find two small pieces of flat wood to make splints.

'Is his leg broken?'

'No. But I need the sticks to keep the dressing in place.'

He found some suitable sticks from the scrub at the side of the road and brought them to her. He watched as she placed the sticks on each side of the wounded leg and bandaged the leg firmly. Blood oozed slowly through the dressing.

'I need to know the time,' said Hannah.

'Why?'

'The bandage should be loosened every hour.'

Mr Cattermole took out a pocket watch from somewhere inside his oilskin jacket. He held it to his ear. 'Stopped,' he said. 'We'll just have to guess.'

Jacka stirred. He opened one eye and then the other. Juno shouted out his name.

Hannah was relieved. 'Give him some water Juno, not too much to begin with.'

Jacka lifted his head and drank a little water. He struggled to his feet and tried to put his weight on his injured back leg. He fell over. Juno stroked his head.

Hannah was worried about the amount of blood seeping through the dressing. If only there was a way to keep the dog still to allow for clots to form. Somewhere safe he could stay until the bleeding stopped.

'I know a place,' said Mr Cattermole. 'Close to here.'

He picked up the dog gently and placed him onto Captain's back. Hannah was surprised that the horse allowed this.

Mr Cattermole lifted Juno up into the saddle and told her to hold on to Jacka. 'Captain will walk slowly. You won't fall off again.'

Hannah did not ask where they were headed. She already knew.

From the moment she first saw it, the white house and its surroundings had attained an almost mythic status for her, an image of perfection that belonged more to the realm of fantasy than reality.

Mr Cattermole said that he did not want to take Captain up the driveway. The metal would play havoc with his shoes. He would rather tether the horse at the gate. Besides, they need to be ready to make a hasty retreat. The willows were thick enough to hide him even in their winter state.

He lifted Jacka from the horse. Hannah checked the dressing on the dog's leg. Blood was still seeping through the bandage although Mr Cattermole said in his opinion the flow had slowed down a little.

He instructed Juno to stay close to Captain. No wandering about.

Hannah said that she felt uneasy about leaving Juno alone at the bottom of the long drive.

'Trust me,' said Mr Cattermole. 'She is safer here by a long shot.'

Mr Cattermole placed Jacka on the canvas sheet. He asked Hannah to carry one side of the sheet to make a secure cradle. Jacka did not try to get out. He lifted his head and sniffed the air. He pricked up his ears and showed some animation when they passed a small flock of sheep grazing in a side paddock.

'Don't even think about it mister,' said Mr Cattermole.

The sheep did not seem to be bothered by the presence of a dog. This, according to Mr Cattermole, was not a good sign. The sheep sensed that the dog was wounded and presented no threat. It could be the end of the line for Jacka.

Mr Cattermole said that there were working dogs kept in cages at the back of the house when it was still a private farm. Maybe Jacka could find temporary shelter there.

They went to the back of the house. The cages were empty. Some of them were locked with rusty padlocks.

Mr Cattermole knocked at the back door. Nobody came. He turned the brass door handle. It did not open. Mr Cattermole said the place was ominously quiet. He hoped like hell that they were not on a wild-goose chase.

Hannah was becoming increasingly anxious. She was worried about Juno all alone at the bottom of the driveway. And she was worried about Jacka. He was lying still with his eyes closed. His breath came out in gentle sighs.

Mr Cattermole knocked at the door again, more loudly this time. A key turned in the lock and the door was opened by a thin woman wearing a white coat and white lace-up shoes.

A bunch of keys hung from her belt. A red wool shawl was flung across her shoulders and pinned at one side with a large cameo brooch. Her hair was pulled back into a bun that was partially covered by a starched white cap.

'Oh it's you,' she said. 'She's not here.'

Mr Cattermole said he was here for the dog. Nothing more.

The woman stared at Hannah. 'And who might you be?'

Mr Cattermole said quickly, 'She's the daughter of a friend.'

'A likely tale,' said the woman. She examined Jacka's leg. 'Needs a cold compress.'

Hannah said that she could make one if she had the right herbs.

'You'd better come in then,' said the woman. 'Bring the dog but keep your voices down. I'm not supposed to have any animals inside.'

She led them into a wide hallway lined with doors, all closed. Halfway down the hall was a burgundy velvet curtain tied back with a tessellated golden rope. She selected a key and opened a door at the end of the hallway. 'My sanctuary,' she said.

Hannah thought that she recognised the tapestry fire screen depicting a hunt in progress, dogs, horses, red jackets and a fox on the run. Had she once shed tears for the fate of this fox? Or was this something that had happened elsewhere?

The woman took out a sheet of unbleached calico from a camphor wood chest and threw it over the sofa. 'Please sit here,' she said. 'Nothing personal, but we have a perennial problem with mud in this place.'

Hannah sat down. Mr Cattermole obeyed without speaking a word. The thin woman rang a bell.

A young woman came into the room. She too was in white with a cap on her head and a red shawl over her shoulders.

She gave a little curtsey to the older woman.

'How can I help?'

'Thank you Nurse Petley. Please take this young lady with you to the dispensary. She desires to make a cold compress to quench a bleeding wound.'

The young nurse asked who the patient was. She was loath to go there without written permission from the Matron.

'Matron has fallen ill as you well know,' said the woman. 'I am in charge here until she returns.'

'Sorry Sister Cattermole, I forgot.' Nurse Petley performed another perfunctory curtsey.

Hannah got to her feet. She followed the nurse down the hallway. She was afraid to ask if Sister Cattermole was related to Wilfred. Perhaps she was an estranged wife. The hostile greeting at the back door had given her a glimpse of a prior history between them.

There were three doors leading off the return veranda. Nurse Petley opened one of them and almost pushed Hannah inside. She locked the door behind them; she seemed to be enjoying herself.

'Now give,' she said. 'Or I won't help you get the herbs you require.'

Hannah stared at her blankly.

'Don't act the innocent with me,' said Nurse Petley. 'It doesn't wash.'

Hannah tried to keep her voice steady. 'Right, I need some crushed garlic and some hedge woundwort.'

Nurse Petley took down an unlabelled jar of herbs from a high shelf.

Hannah removed the lid and sniffed. 'Is this the woundwort?'

'Yes.'

'It looks a bit old. Better than nothing I suppose. Any garlic?'

'Whatever for?'

'It helps to fight infection in the wound.'

'How disgusting.'

'Are there any dried comfrey leaves?'

Nurse Petley said she didn't know where the comfrey was kept. Hannah should go back inside and ask Sister Cattermole. 'But be careful not to rub her up the wrong way. Whenever he turns up, she gets into a bad mood and takes it out on us.'

Hannah said that she would leave well alone. Even without the comfrey, the hedge woundwort should stem the blood flow on Jacka's leg.

'Who's Jacka?'

'Mr Cattermole's dog.'

Nurse Petley's eyes glittered. 'You're kidding. Does Sister Cattermole know that you're treating a dog?'

'She suggested it.'

'Never!'

Hannah hesitated. She wanted to ask Nurse Petley what she meant about acting the innocent. Instead, she thanked her for her help with the herbs.

'Glad to be of assistance,' said the nurse. 'And thanks for the bit of juicy gossip about the dog.'

Juno had obeyed orders and stayed with Captain at the bottom of the drive but by the time Hannah had got to her she was cold and wet and weepy. She said that she had tried to shelter in the willows but some of the old people flew down and threw lumps of ice at her stomach and made the little baby cry.

'It's just hailstones darling,' said Hannah. 'It's safe to go inside now. I'll rub a little butter where it hurts. Soon you will be as good as new.'

'Can I have a bandage like Jacka?'

'Of course.'

Hannah led her gently up the drive. Juno wanted to take her boots off to hear the scrunch of her toes grabbing at the blue metal chips. Hannah said you are the eternal child living in the moment then wished she hadn't because it initiated one of those pointless conversations that culminated in Juno insisting at the top of her voice on having her own way.

Hannah gave in. She helped her sister remove her sodden boots. Juno, triumphant, took a few steps. The stones cut into her bare feet but she did not seem to notice the pain.

Hannah found Mr Cattermole on the back veranda. He frowned when he saw the blood on Juno's feet but made no comment. He asked if Captain was weathering the storm.

Hannah shook her head. 'He's a picture of misery.'

Mr Cattermole said that there was an old shed at the back of the villa. Perhaps Captain could overnight there. The women who run this place had offered them accommodation until the storm blows over. He asked Hannah what she thought.

Hannah, unused to having her opinion sought, said that it was probably safer to stay here than sleep rough in the bush with an injured dog and a pregnant girl. But first, she wanted to ask Mr Cattermole some questions.

'Fire away,' he said. Hannah busied herself with undoing the buttons on Juno's oilskins. 'What is this place?' she asked. 'And who is Sister Cattermole?'

'I'm sorry,' said Mr Cattermole. 'I should have told you sooner. Sister Cattermole is just that, my sister.'

Hannah was immediately on guard. She wondered if she had been tricked into coming here with Juno. Was this a plan cooked up between Mr Cattermole and his sister to hand Juno over to the authorities? She hung the wet oilskins on a peg on the back veranda and tried to stay calm. 'Is this a hospital?'

'More like a private sanatorium. People come here to recover from an illness like the Spanish flu or TB.'

Hannah was somewhat mollified. She agreed that they should stay for one night. But after that, she wanted to leave. She did not feel safe here.

Mr Cattermole left them to attend to his horse.

Hannah opened the back door. The house was cold and dark. She looked down the long hallway. She wondered where the patients were. There was no sign of life except for a chink of light beneath Sister Cattermole's private room.

She took Juno's arm. The girl was shivering. Hannah knocked at the door.

'Come in,' said Sister Cattermole.

Hannah led Juno to the sofa near the fire. The sofa was still covered with the calico sheet. She apologised for the drops of blood coming from Juno's bare feet.

'Oh you poor child,' said Sister Cattermole. 'Come close to the warmth.'

She rang the bell. Nurse Petley appeared instantly as if she was waiting just outside the door. She fetched an enamel bowl with steam rising from it.

'Thank you Nurse,' said Sister Cattermole. 'Leave it with us, we can manage.'

Nurse Petley rattled the door knob and closed the door a little too firmly behind her.

'She means well but she loves to gossip,' said Sister Cattermole. 'And what she doesn't know she invents.'

She carried the bowl to the sofa and kneeling down, lifted Juno's feet gently into the warm water.

Hannah braced herself for Juno's reaction. She did not like to be touched by a stranger. But Juno smiled and cooed like a dove and obligingly lifted one foot and then the other for Sister Cattermole to wash and dry.

'Wilfred filled me in,' said Sister Cattermole. 'About the treatment meted out to the child.'

Hannah said she didn't want to talk about it in front of you-know-who.

'Sorry,' said Sister Cattermole. 'I just want you to know that I disapprove of that hateful committee and everything it stands for.'

She rang the bell again. After a few minutes, Nurse Petley entered the room wheeling a wooden tea trolley. An iron cooking pot sat on the top shelf alongside a china serving dish decorated with delicate pink and green flowers. Plates and utensils were on the bottom shelf.

Nurse Petley announced that Mr Cattermole was in the kitchen warming himself in front of the range. He said not to wait for him.

Sister Cattermole pulled a small drop-leaf table away from the wall. She lifted one side and secured it with a wooden bar. Then she lifted the other side and secured that as well. The rectangular table was now a perfect circle.

Juno clapped her hands. She insisted that Sister Cattermole drop the sides again. And again. It became a game.

'Enough,' said Sister Cattermole at last. 'Time to eat.'

They ate stewed meat from the iron pot. It was slightly stringy but rich in flavour. There was the odd small bone. The china serving dish held a large quantity of mashed potatoes sitting in a warm bath of melted butter. The surface was scored into neat rows with a fork.

Mr Cattermole came into the room. He helped himself to meat and potatoes from the trolley and sat down at the drop-leaf table with the others.

Sister Cattermole asked after the welfare of his horse.

'Snug as a bug in a rug,' said Mr Cattermole.

Juno did not eat much in spite of Hannah's prompting. She could hardly keep her eyes open. Sister Cattermole suggested that Hannah take Juno into room number twelve. Nurse Petley had just finished preparing it for her. Hannah could take the room next door, number eleven.

Hannah said that she would prefer sleeping in the same room as Juno. Nightmares and sleepwalking could be a problem.

'In that case,' said Sister Cattermole, 'Wilfred had better assist us to take another bed into room twelve. There is a spare one in room ten.'

'I don't want to put any of your patients out,' said Mr Cattermole.

Sister Cattermole cleared her throat. 'We're a little bit under capacity at the moment.'

Nurse Petley opened her mouth wide like a fish gasping for air but before she could say anything, Sister Cattermole silenced her with a stern look.

Something shifted in the room, a reminder for Hannah that beneath the warm food and the emerging kindness of Sister Cattermole the possibility of betrayal was ever present.

The comfort she had taken from the external beauty of this place was rapidly turning into despair. She wished that she had never come here. People spoke in riddles. Even Mr Cattermole had changed. He seemed to be afraid of his sister.

Later that night, when Juno had finally succumbed to sleep, Hannah retreated to the bed that Mr Cattermole had wheeled into room twelve. It was little more than a creaky iron cot. The kapok mattress was lumpy and damp. The pillow was covered in unbleached calico with thin blue stripes. It smelt of tobacco smoke and sweat.

Outside the room, the wind howled and shrieked and blew the rain sideways. Hannah was bone tired. She fell into a terrifying dream. Dr Graham's face loomed above her bed like an over-inflated balloon. He denounced her negligence in not discovering Juno's pregnancy earlier. He pretended to smile but the mask fell and he began to plead without moving his lips; *they say that you understand the dark art of necromancy, give me breath girlie, give me the breath of life . . .*

Hannah smashed the bottle of chloroform into his face. Shards of blue glass littered his beard and he fell slowly, like a clumsy dancer, still speaking through closed lips.

The noise of a sheet of corrugated iron banging and thumping on the roof awoke her. The dream had been so vivid that she could almost smell the chloroform.

She lit the candle and checked the contents of her pikau.

The bottle was intact.

Chapter 3

Hannah awoke to an eerie silence. Sometime during the night the storm had decided to leave them in peace. Outside, the only sound was a trickle of water rattling down a broken drain pipe. Runnels of condensation formed by their warm breath drifted down inside the window pane.

Hannah looked across to Juno's bed. The bedding was bunched up. She could not hear her sister breathing. She pulled Juno's bedding aside. The girl had gone.

For a brief moment Hannah wished that Juno had run away into the bush never to return. Grief would come but with it a certain peace.

She tried to stifle these thoughts as soon as they arose. 'Forgive me Juno,' she whispered. 'I'm tired and I'm scared.'

As if on cue the door opened and Juno came in with a breakfast tray loaded with a sugar bowl, a milk jug, a brown teapot, two slices of toast smothered with blackberry jam and an empty cup rattling precariously upon its saucer.

'Made tea, for you.'
'Did someone help you?'
'A nurse did.'
'Which one?'
'Dunno.'

Hannah drank the tepid tea. Juno ate the toast, spitting out the jam seeds against the damp window pane and laughing.

'Did you see Mr Cattermole?' asked Hannah.

'Yep.'

'Did he tell you that we are leaving today?'

'Dunno.'

Hannah said Juno could help her pack their things as soon as they had finished eating.

'Why?' asked Juno.

'So we can leave.'

Out came the lower lip. 'But I like it here.'

Hannah tried the usual diversion of turning a command into a story but Juno would not co-operate.

She went into a state of passive resistance, eyes closed, arms and legs floppy.

Hannah dressed her sister forcibly. She hated doing this but she had no other choice. Juno could keep this up for hours.

The clothes felt damp to the touch. If only she had investigated the cupboard back in the windowless room in Piopio. There may have been some useful items there.

There was a knock on the door. Mr Cattermole entered. Hannah was still wearing her nightgown. He did not seem to notice her embarrassment. He said that they would be leaving very soon. Luckily the rain had stopped but not for long by the look of things.

'Not going,' said Juno.

'Captain is ready,' said Mr Cattermole. 'And Jacka too. We can't leave without you.'

'Not going.'

Mr Cattermole shrugged. 'Okay then. Hannah can ride the horse with Jacka.'

'Jacka wants to stay here.'

'How do you know?' asked Mr Cattermole.

'He told me.'

'You will be all alone. Is that what you want?'

Juno burst into tears.

'Sorry,' said Mr Cattermole. 'I didn't mean to make you cry.'

Hannah sat on the iron bed. She pulled her nightgown down to cover her bare feet. She said that she had something important to ask him. How much money would he need to look after her and Juno? And before he said anything, she knew that her father had paid him to rescue her and Juno from the community.

'Ah this is a delicate matter,' said Mr Cattermole. 'I can't give you an answer at this time and that's the truth.'

'I would pay you if I could.'

'Can we discus this later? Things have become a little more urgent. My sister told me that we must leave at once. She has been reliably informed that a delegation from a certain committee of concerned citizens is on its way.'

Hannah leapt off the bed. She grasped Juno by the shoulders.

'Da da da,' sang Juno.

'No more games. Stay focussed.'

Mr Cattermole took Juno outside and put her on the horse. Hannah packed up as quickly as she could.

Sister Cattermole was waiting at the back door. She gave Hannah two brown paper parcels. 'Roast lamb sandwiches with pickle,' she said.

Hannah apologised for leaving her room in a mess. She had not had time to fold away the bedding or return the dirty dishes to the kitchen.

'Nurse Petley will attend to that. It gives her something to do.'

To Hannah's surprise, Sister Cattermole put her arms around her and gave her a hug. Hannah did not know whether she was expected to reciprocate. She stood awkwardly with her arms at her side until she was released.

'Have a safe journey,' said Sister Cattermole, 'and try to make that child eat more. She barely casts a shadow.'

The horse led by Mr Cattermole appeared at the back veranda with a sulky Juno clinging to the saddle. Jacka sat in front of her, looking much more alert than when Hannah had seen him yesterday.

Sister Cattermole said the dog's recovery was a miracle, no other word would do.

'That is indeed high praise coming from you,' said Mr Cattermole. 'You usually mock those of us who do not have your superior medical wisdom.'

There was an awkward pause. Hannah's mouth went dry. The moment passed.

'Can I leave some of my things here?' asked Mr Cattermole. 'My horse is carrying too much weight.'

Sister Cattermole was reluctant at first but when she saw the shovel and the hatchet that he had uplifted from the side of the road the day before, she took them without further comment.

Mr Cattermole opened one of the saddle bags and pulled out some clothing. Hannah recognised an outfit that she had last seen on a mannequin in her father's shop; tweed jacket, white shirt, cream trousers, and a blue tie.

Sister Cattermole frowned. 'Do these clothes belong to you? If not, I won't be party to such blatant stealing.'

'You took the tools.'

'I need them,' she said.

'Well I need money. I plan to sell them.'

'Just go,' said Sister Cattermole.

Mr Cattermole led the horse down the driveway. Juno, still

sulking, would not respond to any of Hannah's usual tricks to get her out of her bad mood.

They arrived at the roadway. To Hannah's surprise, Mr Cattermole turned left and retraced their steps. She asked him if it was safe to do this. Surely they should have continued along the road that led away from Piopio?

Mr Cattermole said that's what that damned doctor and his so-called moral saviours of the world would expect us to do. But from now on, we are going to undermine their logic at every step. Watch and learn.

Hannah had no option other than to trust him. But who had contacted his sister to pass on a warning? It must have been someone who knew about Juno and her condition.

Mr Cattermole was not particularly forthcoming when she finally found the courage to ask him. 'The fewer people who know anything the better,' he said. 'We could be accused of kidnapping. Or worse.'

Hannah was shaken. Old certainties fell away. It had never occurred to her that rescuing Juno could be construed as illegal.

They moved at a good pace. Mr Cattermole led the horse from the front and Hannah brought up the rear. Soon they left the road and entered what appeared to be thick bush. Juno cried out when a branch of manuka caught the sleeve of her oilskin jacket and ripped a piece of skin from the back of her hand.

The horse stopped. Jacka tried to lick Juno's wound.

'This is not a safe place,' said Hannah.

'You're right,' said Mr Cattermole. 'Only an idiot would bring a horse through here.'

He lifted Jacka from the horse. 'Sorry mate. It's shank's pony from here on.'

Juno wanted to get off the horse too. Mr Cattermole said that he was reluctant to make her walk but there was no alternative. She asked where the other horse was.

'Do you mean Ruby?'

Juno gave him a withering look. 'She's dead.'

'She means the shank's pony,' said Hannah.

Juno went into gales of laughter.

'Sorry,' said Hannah. 'She doesn't mean to be cheeky.'

Mr Cattermole said he didn't mind. It was good to hear her laugh. He suggested that they get moving. He knew of a clearing a few miles away where they could stop and have a break. Juno could help to boil the billy.

Juno clapped her hands. Mr Cattermole lifted her down.

They went deeper into the bush, following an overgrown narrow track. Soon, they came into a relatively open area. Mr Cattermole led Captain to a patch of green grass.

He frowned. 'Someone has grazed a horse here recently. The grass is cropped.'

He led Captain away from the grass and tethered him to the trunk of a matai. 'Don't untie him while I'm gone. He will get the staggers if he eats that ryegrass.'

Juno asked Mr Cattermole where he was going and he said to attend to a call of nature. She asked if she could come too.

Hannah said no. Juno's bottom lip went out.

'We have a job to do,' said Hannah. 'We need dry wood for the fire.'

Mr Cattermole came back. He praised Juno for the small bundle of dry wood she had collected. 'Just a little more,' he said. 'And see if there is any whitey-wood.'

He took some newspaper from a saddle pack and broke some pieces of matai bark into nuggets. Soon he had a small fire going.

Hannah drank tea and ate one of the lamb sandwiches that Sister Cattermole had given them. Mr Cattermole said that the discovery of someone else's horse coming through this track bothered him. And it wasn't just the horse. He said that if you look closely you can see that the undergrowth has been recently cut back with a machete.

Hannah asked him why it worried him.

'Some of the locals are fearful of the history of this place. It was once an old Māori track that served as an escape route during tribal conflict.'

'Are we breaking a rule by coming here?'

'It means that certain other people might know that the track is relatively open and come looking for us.'

Juno was conducting a one-sided conversation with Captain. She put her face against his and giggled when she felt the tickle of his eyelashes against her forehead.

'There's been a change of plan,' said Mr Cattermole. 'We must leave right now.'

Hannah hurriedly packed away the remaining food. Mr Cattermole gulped down the last of the billy tea and threw the damp leaves deep into the bush.

Juno said that she wanted to go to the little house. She had found it first, it belonged to her. Mr Cattermole said that the raupo hut was not safe. Too many people knew that he sometimes went there when he was searching for lost sheep.

Mr Cattermole covered the fire with lumps of damp clay and checked the clearing for any signs of their brief habitation.

'Let's go,' he said.

They re-commenced their journey. Hannah was thankful that Mr Cattermole's prediction of the return of the rain did not eventuate. The dense bush gradually gave way to more open country. Mr Cattermole said that they were now descending towards the coast.

They came upon a swollen creek. Drowned willows clung to the banks, fighting against a tide of angry green water. Mr Cattermole said oh bugger beneath his breath.

'Going to tell on you,' said Juno.

'You've got the sharpest ears around,' said Mr Cattermole.

'Are we going to ford this creek?' asked Hannah.

Mr Cattermole said that had been the plan. But now they must retrace their steps a little. There is an abandoned settler's house somewhere along this route. He had not been this far across country for ages so it may have finally given up the ghost.

Mr Cattermole led Captain to higher ground away from the swollen creek. Jacka limped behind. Juno began to snivel. Hannah recognised this cry. It was usually a precursor to a full-blown crying fit, a fit of the bellows as Sarah called it, no tears, just a noise like a wounded beast emerging from the depths of an imagined forest.

The afternoon light began to slip towards a sepia dusk. Juno was still snivelling, but to Hannah's relief, her vocalisations had not progressed into an attack of the bellows.

There was no sign of human habitation except for rotting fence posts and spindly trees covered with lichen marking out abandoned orchards.

They rested for a while, Juno silent at last.

'Where are we?' asked Hannah.

'I don't know,' said Mr Cattermole. 'But I bet Jacka does.'

As if on cue, Jacka lifted his head and sniffed the air. He hobbled along for a minute, then turned and sat down on his haunches, waiting for them to catch up.

'I hope this is not a false alarm,' said Mr Cattermole.

Juno said that Jacka was using his blue eye as a torch to light their way. See how it shines. Like a paua shell.

Mr Cattermole said that could be a poem. Juno said not really because it doesn't rhyme. What does shell go with? Mr Cattermole said hell, it rhymes with hell and Juno burst into tears.

'I should have warned you,' said Hannah. 'She is very frightened of that word.'

Jacka led them to the top of a rise. He waved his tail like a black-and-white banner then lay down with his head resting on his paws.

'He's found the settler's hut,' said Mr Cattermole. 'I recognise the terrain. It's down in a gully and it's quite steep. You take care of Juno and I'll lead the horse down.'

Juno dried her tears and with a sudden burst of energy, zigzagged down the narrow ridges formed by the feet of feral sheep.

'Slow down, slow down!' cried Hannah.

'The girl is surprisingly agile,' said Mr Cattermole.

Hannah tried to stay calm. She was afraid that her sister would meet with an accident, but when they arrived at the bottom, Juno was waiting, safe and sound.

The settler's shack was well camouflaged by a stand of regenerating bush at the base of the gully. Mamaku ferns with jet-black trunks thrust their green lacy umbrellas above clumps of juvenile tarata and kanuka.

Through the gathering gloom of the encroaching night, Hannah had a fleeting glimpse of the settler's shack, a slab hut made out of split timber topped by white pine tiles. She was overcome with a shock of recognition. This hut was a replica of some of the early buildings back at the settlement. Had she been miraculously transported back to a mirror image of the place that she had just left?

Mr Cattermole said he would never have found the shack if Jacka had not remembered the exact location.

'That dog is worth his weight in lamb shanks,' he said.

He opened the door of the shack. Something scuttled away in the corner.

'A rat!' sang Juno, 'a big fat rat!'

'Stay outside until I've worked out what the hell is going on,' said Mr Cattermole.

'What's wrong?' said Hannah.

'Everything,' answered Mr Cattermole.

White light began to flow out of the hut into the darkening night. Mr Cattermole said it was now safe to come in; he had managed to get the paraffin lamp going.

Hannah and Juno came into the room. Mr Cattermole replaced the glass chimney on the mantel lamp. It burned with a pure clean light.

Hannah looked around the room. It was immaculate. The clay floor was smooth and hard and shiny. Tins of food were stacked neatly on a shelf next to the fireplace. A large wicker basket containing small logs for the fire sat on the other side. Wood ash was spread evenly beneath an iron colonial oven sitting on a row of bricks on the hearth. There was the unmistakable yeasty smell of recently baked bread.

'This is serious,' said Mr Cattermole. 'Someone knew we were coming.'

'But that's impossible,' said Hannah. 'We did not have a plan. And even if we did, the flooded creek forced us to change the direction of our journey.'

Mr Cattermole took a small piece of paper from the wicker basket and placed it on the ashes beneath the colonial oven. It smouldered for a minute then burst into flame.

'Thought so,' he said. 'Those ashes are fresh.'

Juno said she was hungry. The little baby was growling at her from the inside.

Mr Cattermole said he was hungry too. He rummaged around in his pikau and pulled out a torn shirt. He wrapped the shirt around his hand and took the lid off the colonial oven. 'Ouch!' he cried. He dropped the lid with a clatter.

Inside lay a white loaf, beautifully risen, smothered in poppy seeds. The centre of the loaf was decorated with rosettes and plaited strips of dough.

Hannah was suspicious but she was starving so she put her fears aside while they ate.

They tore at the bread ravenously.

Jacka slid quietly inside, head down, legs moving very slowly. Juno gave him a chunk of the warm bread. He wolfed it down.

'You'll make him sick,' said Mr Cattermole. 'Dogs are meant to eat meat.'

'There isn't none,' said Juno.

Hannah, her mouth full of warm bread, said look up, there's a safe hanging up from the roof. Wind it down and look inside.

Mr Cattermole said that Jacka should not be inside the hut. He is a working dog pure and simple. But in spite of what he said, he pulled down the rope that attached the safe to the roof and showed Juno the special mesh door that kept the flies at bay.

Juno opened the safe and took out a large bone with meat and sinews hanging from it.

Jacka sat very still, staring at the meat as if it were live prey about to take flight.

'It's a bit whiffy, said Mr Cattermole, 'but Jacka won't mind. Take it outside for him, there's a good girl.'

He rolled a cigarette and lit it with a burning taper from the ashes. He whispered something that Hannah could barely hear. He beckoned her to come closer. She obeyed. 'What do you make of all this,' he asked.

She said that they had probably walked into a trap. She wanted to leave right now.

'Everything that we need is provided, beds, blankets, food, warmth,' said Mr Cattermole. 'We have to spend at least one night here. We have no choice.'

'But who has done this? Perhaps the preparation is meant to be for someone else.'

Mr Cattermole said that this was highly unlikely. There were certain clues that only he could pick up. Like the bread. For a short period in his past life he had lived on such loaves, an exact replica to the one that they had just devoured. Only one person could bake this loaf to perfection in such an oven.

He rolled up another cigarette. Hannah noticed that his hands were trembling. He mumbled something, a name. She asked Mr Cattermole to repeat it. He placed the unlit cigarette behind his ear and said more clearly this time, 'Eleanor, your mother.'

Hannah was surprised, then wary. 'She made this bread?'

'Well if not her, someone who knew how to make a perfect loaf in a colonial oven.'

Hannah kept her voice light. 'Did you have much to do with her?'

'We all did, Lena, my sister, and of course your father,' said Mr Cattermole.

He said that he had never since seen any likeness of Eleanor. Not a photo or a painting. He's not sure if he wanted to. Better to keep the past where it belongs.

Hannah was afraid that if she asked him too many questions he would take refuge once again behind his wall of silence. She took the risk. 'If my mother made the bread, then she must be alive?'

'That depends on who you talk to,' said Mr Cattermole. He hesitated. 'Is this difficult for you?'

Hannah nodded.

'I'm sorry I can't tell you more. The truth is I don't know. We all have our theories about Eleanor. In a strange kind of way that's all she has become.'

'What do you mean?'

'All of us tell different stories about her. Take my sister. According to her, I became the villain of the piece years ago and made Eleanor lose her mind.'

'Was this before or after Eleanor abandoned me and Juno?'

Mr Cattermole took the cigarette from behind his ear and twisted each end. 'Abandoned is too strong a word. She thought it better to leave both of you in a Christian community rather than at the mercy of Charlie Cooper or the state. She had no idea that years later the real threat would come from within the community.'

'Do you mean Jimmy?'

'Yes, and possibly others.'

There was a commotion outside. A horse whinnied. It did not sound like Captain.

Jacka arrived at the open door, panting. He hobbled inside, favouring his wounded leg. He butted Mr Cattermole's thigh with his head.

'What is it boy?'

Hannah heard a faint cry from outside. Juno was pleading with someone to leave her alone.

Hannah ran out of the door, followed by Mr Cattermole and Jacka. All was calm and still. Had she imagined Juno's plea for help?

'Did you tether Captain?' asked Mr Cattermole.

'No.'

'Someone did.'

Hannah looked up the slope of the gully. There was no sign of Juno or a strange horse. Whoever had whisked her away had left no trace.

'Where the devil did she get to?' said Mr Cattermole. 'Jacka seek, seek.'

Jacka tried to run up the sheep tracks, then stopped and looked back at Mr Cattermole.

'Juno! Juno!' called Hannah. 'I'm here, I'm here!'

'Stay calm,' said Mr Cattermole. 'She can't have gone far.'

Hannah shivered. Jacka came back down the slope and pushed his wet muzzle into her crotch. She patted him on the head. 'It's not your fault boy.'

Mr Cattermole said they must find Juno before the cold night air came barrelling down the hill. He instructed Hannah to stay within the hut and put plenty of wood on the fire. She must not worry. Juno will probably be able to find her own way back.

'She plays a game sometimes,' said Hannah.

'What game?'

'Hide and seek.'

'This is no time for playing games,' said Mr Cattermole. 'How can she be so thoughtless?'

Hannah wanted to say that he was beginning to sound just like the others who initially felt sorry for Juno and then made judgments about her as if she were an ordinary girl. But she said nothing. The immediate task was to find her sister.

Mr Cattermole buttoned up his oilskin jacket and put a flashlight, a water bottle and the last crust of white bread into his pikau. Soon Hannah was alone with the warm glow from the paraffin lamp and the flickering fire.

Jacka lay down on the wooden step, half in, half out, keeping the door of the hut ajar. Although this meant that cold air crept into the hut, Hannah ordered him to stay where he was. He was her sentinel, a watch dog in the true sense of the word.

She turned over the smouldering embers beneath the colonial oven and fed the fire with the logs in the wicker basket.

Mr Cattermole had said something very important about her abandonment. Hannah clung to his words like a lifeline, but she wanted more. She was hungry for the tiniest clue about Eleanor's past life and her current whereabouts.

Jacka lifted his head. Was the dog telling her something? Hannah listened carefully. Nothing.

Jacka stood up and stared at her, his one blue eye intense and unblinking. Then, in spite of his injured leg he took off. Hannah chased him for what felt like hours. She did her best to avoid the prickly undergrowth that strayed across the edges of the track.

Jacka stopped suddenly. Further along the track Hannah saw Juno's thin bare legs sticking out beneath a low stand of silver fern.

Jacka inched forward on his stomach then took to his feet. He reached Juno just before Hannah did.

Juno sat up and put her arms around the dog. Jacka licked her face.

Hannah was overwhelmed with relief.

'I ran away cos a horse reared up at me,' said Juno. 'A white horse, with wings.'

'Don't you ever run away from me again!'

Juno stuck her bottom lip out.

Hannah felt contrite. She was doing the very thing that she had condemned in others. She was treating Juno as if she were an ordinary girl.

Hannah could not take the bottom-lip treatment much longer. She decided to go into Juno's madness with her, just for a little while. She cradled Juno in her arms and felt a powerful kick from the child within her.

A whirlwind of fear twisted her gut. The prospect of her sister coming through a long childbirth unscathed was almost unimaginable. She was small for her age and fragile to the bone.

Hannah had assisted in childbirths in the community but they had been to adult women who had birthed before. Even then, the suffering had been intolerable. The rule of the community was that women in childbirth must remain completely silent to atone for Eve's original sin.

Hannah consoled herself with the knowledge that the small blue bottle of chloroform and the Skinner mask lay hidden at the bottom of her pikau. She would be able to send Juno into a light sleep when the fateful day came.

Hannah helped her sister to her feet. Juno asked her if she had seen the white horse with wings.

'Of course I did my darling.'

Juno beamed. 'The other lady did too.'

'Hush now,' said Hannah. 'We need to get back to the hut. Put your arms around my neck and hold on tight.'

A gibbous moon riding high behind the threaded clouds produced an illusion of a flickering celestial lantern. Jacka, now limping badly, led the way.

The track seemed longer and more tortuous on the way back. There were side tracks that branched off the main track that Hannah could not remember seeing in her blind panic to find Juno. She stopped at one crossroad uncertain whether to turn left or right.

Jacka lay down, rested his head on his front paws and closed his eyes.

'Please don't give up on us.' said Hannah.

'Da da da,' sang Juno.

Jacka pricked up his ears.

'Keep singing Juno,' said Hannah. 'He's listening.'

Jacka got to his feet. He trotted off to the right.

Juno said we can't go there. The lady said not to.

Hannah said we must trust the dog. We have no choice.

Jacka led them to a wider part of the track. Hannah almost wept with relief when she recognised some of the features of the regenerating bush.

Hannah hoped Mr Cattermole would be waiting for them with a hot cup of tea and would praise her for finding her lost sister.

But he was not there.

Something had changed. The hut was withdrawing into itself; the fire had gone out, empty tins had been dropped onto the clay floor. She touched the glass chimney of the paraffin lamp. It was cold.

Hannah ordered Jacka to guard the doorway. She tried to relight the fire without success. She shivered. How long had she and Juno been away? And where was Mr Cattermole?

Juno said that she was tired. Hannah wrapped her in a blanket that lay folded neatly on the wooden bunk. There were holes in the blanket that Hannah had not noticed before. Juno mumbled big fat rats then closed her eyes and went into a deep sleep.

Hannah spent most of the night trying to come to grips

with the fact that Mr Cattermole had not returned to the hut. She resented the fact that he had left her in this alien place. Nothing seemed solid anymore. A place that had promised sanctuary had abruptly withdrawn its munificence.

And why had Mr Cattermole taken the last of the tinned food with him? She did not remember seeing him put anything in his pikau except for his flashlight, a bottle of water and a crust of bread. Had he hidden the other tins outside the shack?

She had no idea what she should do. Would it be safer for them to leave the hut and try to retrace their tracks back to the white villa? In spite of Sister Cattermole's acerbic tongue, she would not turn them away. Or at least Hannah hoped that this would be the case.

At last Hannah drifted off to sleep, a merciful respite. She awoke just at that turning point in the night when the sky darkens before dawn, pitch black and silent. The moon, a shadow of its former self, was caught in the act of slipping down the steep side of the gully.

Hannah felt abandoned. Even the moon was leaving her. And where was Jacka? She had told him to guard the doorway. At least Juno was still asleep. The poor child must have been exhausted.

She saw the dog before she heard him. He was a picture of abject misery. He slunk in the door and flopped to the floor. Someone had tied a rope to his collar. The end of the rope was frayed and covered in dirt.

Hannah could not stem her tears. Her sobs woke Juno.

She tickled Hannah's face with the fringe of the blanket. Hannah started to giggle and Juno joined her. Once they had started, they could not stop.

Jacka joined in with copious licking of faces and hands.

None of them noticed the doorway darkening a little in the early morning light.

Hannah was the first to see the shadow. She grasped Jacka's collar. He did not react except for thumping his tail vigorously on the clay floor.

Juno stopped laughing. So did Hannah.

A woman's voice commanded Jacka to lie down and be still and the dog obeyed.

The woman held out her hands. Hannah already knew what she would see; a crushed finger nail and a ragged purple scar that looked like the head of a dog.

'I see you recognise this,' said the woman. 'My passport to hell and back.'

The dawn light struggled down into the gully. The noises of the bush were suspended as if lying in wait for the next player to arrive. There was no birdsong.

Hannah found it difficult to come to grips with the physical presence of Eleanor. She would never have recognised her from the photos that Sarah had given her. The lustrous white skin that once shone like a pearl was muddied and dark.

Eleanor could not stop staring at Hannah. She put her hand out and tried to touch her. The two women, mother and child, circled each other like wary cats.

In the end it was Eleanor who broke down. She wept, she cursed, she berated herself out loud for leaving her two girls in such a place where mirrors are forbidden and women are nothing but pack horses and servants of the men.

Juno sat on the wooden bunk picking rat holes in the blanket.

'Leave that blanket alone,' said Hannah.

'Leave that blanket alone,' parroted Juno.

Juno pushed her bottom lip out. She looked at Eleanor for comfort. None came.

Hannah could not help herself. She was totally in love. She wanted to touch Eleanor's long skirt, ragged at the edges, smelling of a mixture of swamp water and the urine of horses. She wanted to crawl inside her mother's body.

She could barely speak. She was desperate to give Eleanor a good impression of her but there were no appropriate words. She wished that she could offer Eleanor some food and a hot drink but the shelves were bare.

'Would you like me to light the fire?' asked Eleanor.

She opened a stained canvas bag that looked like a saddle pack. It smelt of rich leaf mould. She put her scarred hand down the side and pulled out a neatly folded newspaper. Soon she had a cheerful blaze going in the brick fireplace. The damp wood hissed a little but soon gave up its moisture to her expert hands.

Juno was subdued. She sat on the bunk with her back to the two women.

Eleanor took some calico bags from her pack. She held up one that had the words *Lily White Flour* stencilled in red. She toned her voice down to a whisper. 'Does she eat the same stuff that we do?'

Hannah nodded. She watched her in fascination. She had never seen a woman work so quickly and so skilfully. Eleanor asked if there was any oatmeal.

Juno broke her silence. 'Big fat rats, big fat rats,' she sang.

Eleanor stopped kneading the bread. 'My god, the child has a voice. Does she always sing so sweetly?'

Hannah nodded. She did not feel in the mood to discuss Juno with Eleanor. She wanted her mother's full attention. She wanted answers and she wanted them now.

Eleanor placed the bread into the colonial oven. She said

that she had made soda bread because she had run out of yeast. She asked when Wilfred was expected back. He must be hungry by now.

Hannah was immediately put on her guard. How did Eleanor know that Mr Cattermole had brought them here? And why did she call him by his first name?

Her mother was proving to be as slippery as an eel. What had Mr Cattermole said about her? *We all have our theories about Eleanor. In a strange kind of way that's all she has become.*

Eleanor went outside to fetch some rainwater from a bucket at the side of the door. She pulled a pannikin from the canvas bag, filled it with water, and placed it on the top of the colonial stove. She produced a tin containing fruit cake from her seemingly bottomless bag. Soon they were drinking hot tea.

Juno gave up sulking and wolfed down a hunk of cake.

'That's enough for now,' said Hannah. 'Leave some for later.'

Juno patted her stomach. 'The little baby is hungry,' she said.

'So it's true,' said Eleanor. 'There is to be a child.'

The two women went outside. Eleanor sat on a fallen log at the front of the settler's shack and rolled up a cigarette. 'What's going on? All I have is a garbled account from Sarah.'

Hannah was surprised to hear mention of Sarah. She asked Eleanor if she had been to the settlement.

'Only once, that dreadful day when I had to leave you and Juno there. I have kept track of you through Sarah. We sometimes meet secretly in Piopio. It has become more difficult of late. Sarah is becoming too frail to make the journey.'

'I have to know why you are here,' said Hannah.

Eleanor took a deep drag on her cigarette. 'The powers that be want to make Juno a State Ward and put her into an orphanage.'

'It's even worse than that now,' said Hannah. 'Our father has become president of the eugenics society. They want to kill the baby and cut Juno open and put her into an asylum.'

'I hoped to god this wouldn't happen. I once saw one of those places. Full of fearful mad children chained to the wall, punished for bed wetting, beaten up, confused. I swear Juno will never be put into a place like that.'

'Really?' said Hannah. 'You've abandoned us before.'

Eleanor stubbed out her cigarette. 'I never intended for you to be in that dreadful community so long. But Sarah told me that you were both well settled and that you had become a healer.'

Hannah said they had been settled, but everything became unravelled when Mr Cattermole showed up almost dead in the river.

'Tell me everything that has happened,' said Eleanor.

Hannah hesitated. She remembered Mr Cattermole saying that everyone had a particular theory of what made Eleanor tick. Perhaps her mother was pretending to be remorseful for her own purposes.

'Come on,' said Eleanor. 'Don't be afraid, you have done nothing wrong. We must move quickly.'

Hannah was once again on the edge of the river. This time there was no dead body, just the movement of water plummeting cleanly through the tangled willows.

She started slowly, then spoke faster and faster, each word tumbling over the next.

With each disclosure, Eleanor became more visibly agitated.

Hannah touched her on the shoulder. Eleanor leaned towards her and Hannah found herself taking her in her arms and comforting her.

Juno called from the doorway of the shack. 'The bread is cooked.'

'Don't let her see your tears,' said Hannah.

Eleanor wiped her face with her shawl. 'You have looked after your poor sister much better than I could ever have done.'

Hannah went back into the shack and helped Juno retrieve the loaf from the oven.

'Now watch,' said Hannah. 'This is how you test the loaf to see if it's cooked right through.' She turned the bread upside down and the tin slid away. She knocked on the bottom of the loaf. It sounded hollow.

'We've done well,' said Hannah. 'It's ready to eat.'

Eleanor appeared at the doorway. 'I think we have a visitor,' she said. She grabbed her canvas bag and put it beneath the blanket on the wooden bunk.

Hannah heard a voice, faint at first, then two voices becoming louder and clearer. One of the voices belonged to Mr Cattermole.

'It's Dr Graham,' said Eleanor, 'the one who wants to take Juno away. What the hell is Wilfred playing at?'

Hannah wanted to grab Juno and make a run for it. 'Come with us,' she begged.

Eleanor shook her head. 'No time for that,' she said. 'We have to take control of the situation. When I heard Juno was pregnant I thought this might happen. I have just the thing we need.'

'Some swine has stolen my horse,' shouted Dr Graham. 'I paid a bloody fortune for it.'

'Language please,' said Mr Cattermole. He knocked on the

door jamb. 'May we enter?'

'Wait a minute,' said Eleanor. 'I'm not dressed yet.'

Mr Cattermole did not appear to be surprised at the presence of Eleanor. 'We'll go and look for the horse then,' said Mr Cattermole. 'Back soon.'

Eleanor took a comb from a small bag hidden beneath her bodice and ran it through her hair. She powdered her face and applied bright red lipstick with a fine brush. She drew two perfect eyebrows with a black pencil and smudged some kohl onto the lids of her eyes.

Hannah was impressed at the rapid transformation that Eleanor had achieved without the use of a mirror. Eleanor said she functioned better when she had her war paint on.

Outside, the men were calling to the lost horse.

Juno said that she saw it flying up towards the stars. Should she go outside and tell them about the wings?

'Forget the horse,' said Eleanor. 'Both of you come close. Whatever I say to these men, keep silent. Say nothing. I need to tell some big lies and it helps if you just nod your head when I ask you questions.'

She opened the canvas pack and withdrew something wrapped in a dirty white towel. She unfolded the towel, revealing an opaque glass jar filled with smoky liquid. There was something floating in the liquid, a tiny creature with arms and feet and a bulbous head.

'From now on,' said Eleanor, 'this is where your little baby lives.'

Juno began to sob. Eleanor said don't get upset. The little creature in the glass jar was not Juno's, it belonged to another lady. But we need to use it so that those men will leave us alone.

Hannah felt sick. Eleanor must be deluded if she thought

that Dr Graham would fall for this. But Eleanor was adamant that it would work.

Juno dried her tears. She took the jar and held it tightly to her chest. 'Is the little baby sad?'

Eleanor said that she likes floating in her special swimming pool, wriggling her toes and fingers, forever young.

Hannah heard the clop of a horse approaching. Juno wanted to go outside to see if the men had found the white horse but Hannah restrained her.

'Keep holding onto the jar Juno,' said Eleanor. 'Don't let anyone take it away from you.'

Mr Cattermole came into the hut without knocking. 'Any chance of a brew? I'm parched.'

'So that's all you want from me after all this time,' said Eleanor.

Mr Cattermole said sorry. The gravity of the situation had made him forget his manners. He had tried everything to stop Dr Graham coming to look for Juno. The man had become obsessed with his wretched eugenics society.

Eleanor told him not to talk about such things in front of the girls.

'Sorry,' he said again.

Hannah, keeping her voice as steady as possible, asked him if Dr Graham had found his horse.

Mr Cattermole frowned. 'Yes and no.'

'You haven't changed much,' said Eleanor. 'You still enjoy being enigmatic.'

'We found a horse all right but Graham said it wasn't his.'

'The man is a fool,' said Eleanor.

Mr Cattermole lowered his voice. 'Don't underestimate him Eleanor.'

Eleanor removed the lid from an iron kettle from the top

of the colonial oven and threw a handful of tea leaves into the boiling water.

Mr Cattermole tried to be jovial. He rubbed his hands together and said how nice it was to see the two girls reunited with their mother. After all these years, who would have thought that Eleanor could look so beautiful.

Her mother's painted face began to melt in the hot air of the stove. Her left eye looked as if she had recently been a participant in a fight. She sat down next to Mr Cattermole on the wooden bench close to the fire. 'It is so cosy here,' he said. 'If things were different, it could be a nice place to come to in the summer.'

She said that she had something very sad to tell him. 'Last night when you went missing, poor little Juno lost the baby.'

Mr Cattermole said, 'Oh how terrible but perhaps . . .'

'Don't you dare say it's all for the best.'

'Given the circumstances,' said Mr Cattermole, 'what else is there to say?'

'The poor child is in shock.'

Juno was giving the performance of her life. Trembling, with her eyes closed, she looked the picture of impossible grief.

Mr Cattermole asked if he could take a look at the foetus. Juno refused to remove the towel wrapped around the glass jar.

Hannah, fighting her own demons, found it difficult to participate in the charade.

Eleanor sliced some of the hot soda bread. Mr Cattermole ate ravenously.

Eleanor asked Mr Cattermole if Dr Graham would come to the shack now that he had found his horse.

Mr Cattermole said it depends on whether he accepts the

stray horse as his.

Eleanor confessed that she had stolen his horse. When she saw him in the bush she had guessed he was looking for Juno and wanted to stall him.

'I'll whistle up Jacka. Have you seen him?'

'Yes. And he recognised me. After all this time.'

Hannah took a piece of soda bread to Juno. She signalled with her eyes that she was proud of her. Juno was obeying Eleanor to the letter.

Mr Cattermole said, 'What is your plan? Juno should have medical attention at once.'

Eleanor said sharply 'You are forgetting who you are talking to. I have delivered more babies than you've had hot dinners.'

'Sorry,' said Mr Cattermole.

Hannah almost broke Eleanor's instruction not to query anything. Later, she thought, later I will question her. Please god she is telling the truth about her experience as a midwife.

'The most urgent thing is to get rid of Dr Graham,' said Mr Cattermole. 'For good.'

He went to the door of the shack and whistled for Jacka to come. The dog arrived limping.

'Stay,' commanded Mr Cattermole. Jacka sank down on the long grass near the doorway of the hut.

Outside, the air was crystal clear. There was a sound of a horse whinnying and clopping along in the gully.

'Ah,' said Mr Cattermole. 'That is not Captain, it must be the elusive white horse.'

Jacka gave a warning growl.

'Enemy approaching,' said Mr Cattermole.

They sat in silence until the doctor arrived. He stepped over the reclining dog, carrying his saddle in one hand and his whip in the other. 'Where the bloody hell did you get to Cattermole?'

'Sit down Doctor,' said Eleanor. 'And watch your language in front of my daughters.'

Dr Graham dropped his whip. 'For god's sake woman, you frightened the tripes out of me.' He peered at her. 'Is it really you?'

Eleanor changed her tactics. She became all sweetness and light. She gushed over Dr Graham, offered him tea and the last crust of soda bread. There may even be a slice of fruit cake left.

Dr Graham kissed the back of her good hand. 'You look exactly the same. How many years since I last saw you?'

Hannah peered though the dim light of the shack. Her mother's eyes were almost black, her head high and proud. She marvelled at Eleanor's ability to slide from one identity to another.

'Thank goodness you are here,' Eleanor said in a low silky voice. 'Juno and Hannah are naughty girls for running away from you and their father. I blame Lena and this so-called gentleman sitting not too far away from you for egging them on.'

Dr Graham dunked the crust of bread into his tea and sucked it dry. 'No harm done. Just ask the girls to pack up their things.'

'What about the horse?' asked Mr Cattermole.

Dr Graham looked foolish. He admitted that it was his horse after all.

'There are five of us,' said Mr Cattermole. 'Too many riders.'

At this moment, Juno, right on cue, let out an ungodly shriek.

The doctor dropped his cup on the wooden bench. Jacka

lifted up his muzzle and howled like a wolf. Eleanor rushed to the bunk and held Juno in her arms. Juno kept on shrieking while Jacka produced another canine cadenza from his limited repertoire.

'Do something for Christ's sake,' said Dr Graham. 'My head is going in and out.'

Hannah sent a signal to Juno. The noise stopped as suddenly as it had started.

Jacka tried one last high note but missed his mark and emitted a squeak.

'Peace at last,' said Dr Graham. 'They could wake the dead between them.'

Eleanor said if only that was true. There had been a death last night, right here, in this god-forsaken place.

The doctor looked startled. 'Who died?'

'Just an unwanted child,' said Mr Cattermole.

Eleanor put her fingers to her lips. 'Hush now, don't upset Juno. She's grieving.'

The doctor shook his head. 'A miscarriage? I find that hard to believe.'

Eleanor led him to the bunk. She asked Juno to remove the dirty towel from the glass jar. Juno, somewhat reluctantly, obeyed.

Hannah peered into the jar. Juno gave it a gentle shake. The liquid had become less opaque. It was easy to see the eyeless creature turning slowly, so prettily, like a sea horse coming up for air.

Dr Graham frowned. 'It looks intact, but she will have to come to Taumarunui Hospital for a curette just to make sure it all came away.'

Eleanor said she wanted to make sure that Juno would be safe from infection. Where better than a hospital?

'I'm so glad that you have come around to my way of thinking,' said the doctor.

'Tell you what,' said Mr Cattermole. 'I'll stay with the girls so that Juno can recover. She's not ready for a bumpy horse ride. You two can go on ahead.'

The doctor was wary of this plan until Eleanor said that she thought it was a good idea. She would accompany him, just to show her good will and her heartfelt thanks for helping Juno.

Mr Cattermole said he could track down a konaki to bring the girls to the hospital. Then Hannah and Juno could ride like royalty snug as a bug through the mud and muck of the bush roads.

After another cup of tea and the last of the fruit cake, Eleanor packed a few things in her pikau and announced that she was ready to leave.

Dr Graham fussed over Eleanor, making sure that she was comfortable on the saddle. He adjusted the stirrups and tightened the girth by taking up another notch on the second strap to even it up with the first. He said that he would walk until they were out of the bush. There was a cleared track down the line on the way to Piopio where they could double-up. Eleanor was so tiny that the horse would barely notice the extra weight.

Hannah and Mr Cattermole waved to them.

'Goodbye darling girls,' said Eleanor. 'Be good.'

Hannah washed the cups and plates in warm water from the kettle. Juno stayed on the bunk bed pretending to cry. Hannah told Juno that she was proud of her but she could dry her tears now. She had done exactly what Eleanor had asked her to do.

'Now what?' asked Mr Cattermole.

'I thought you had a plan,' said Hannah, a little stiffly.

'Do you think that the doctor was fooled? Or was he glad to be shot of the whole business?'

'I have no idea.'

'Don't get snaky with me,' said Mr Cattermole. 'I'm only trying to help.'

'Snaky snaky snaky,' said Juno.

'I don't believe that the foetus was fresh, not for a minute,' said Mr Cattermole. 'Where, for a start, did Eleanor get hold of formaldehyde way out here at the back of beyond?'

'She might have had some stored away in her canvas saddle-bag.'

'Highly unlikely. Besides, there's something I want you to see. Come over here and have a look.'

But Juno didn't want to relinquish her hold on the jar.

Hannah took control and removed it gently. 'It doesn't belong to us. We have to give it back.'

'That would be impossible,' said Mr Cattermole. 'It has travelled a long way.'

He pointed out an inscription on a tiny plaque on the side of the jar. He read the words aloud. *Property of Otago Medical School. Not to be Removed.*

Juno said it was sad that the little baby had to stay locked away in a jar.

Mr Cattermole thought it a huge joke. 'Eleanor has a lot of nerve!' he said, laughing. 'Where the hell did she get this from?'

Hannah said she failed to see anything funny about the situation.

'I shouldn't doubt her,' said Mr Cattermole, Eleanor knows what she's doing. 'She has that idiot exactly where she wants him, and she will win, mark my words.'

Hannah thought yes and she's got to you too. But she said

nothing in spite of her desire to question him about his past relationship with her mother. She knew that in spite of this need, she would find it almost impossible to bring it up in conversation, either with him or her mother.

Her resentment grew. Here she was again, in a frightening situation with a tenuous grasp of what motivated the other players. Juno on the other hand was an open book to her. This was all very well but how on earth could she protect her sister when she, Hannah, had so little understanding of how other people live.

I am useless she thought. I am a blank slate that has yet to be exposed to the world. This thought was still on her mind when she awoke to the sound of wind and rain lashing the ferns that clung to their meagre shelter.

Mr Cattermole wanted to make a move but he had to track down a konaki. The storm blew sharp and cold and they were forced to stay inside the shack until the weather improved.

The next day Hannah was reluctant to leave her refuge. She did not believe that the storm had abated. Juno too complained about leaving her bunk, the place where she spent most of her time. She had suddenly ballooned up and found it difficult to eat. Her fragile ankles were swollen.

There was now plenty of food on offer. Mr Cattermole went off with Jacka at dawn to shoot a rabbit and the tinned food that had mysteriously disappeared a few days ago had come back with added abundance.

Hannah mentioned that disturbing day when she had seen the hut withdraw into itself; food was there one moment, the next, it was gone.

Mr Cattermole was sitting on an improvised seat he had made from the trunk of a juvenile kahikatea.

He rolled up a cigarette. 'Perhaps it was Eleanor up to her

old tricks.'

Hannah did not answer him. She busied herself preparing a pile of twigs she was breaking up for the fire. The kindling was wet and needed to be placed on the top of the oven to dry out.

'You can be frustrating at times,' said Mr Cattermole.

Hannah snapped another piece of manuka with excessive force.

'Just like your mother,' he said. 'Cat got your tongue?'

Hannah was becoming increasingly annoyed with him. He was trying to get a reaction from her.

He must have sensed her mood because he changed the subject by calling out to Juno to bring the carcass of the rabbit he had shot that morning and give the ears and the paws to Jacka for a treat.

Juno said she was too tired and her feet wouldn't work any more.

'But Jacka wants you,' said Mr Cattermole.

'For goodness sake leave the child alone,' said Hannah.

Meanwhile, Juno was complaining about the whereabouts of the tongue-stealing cat, and no amount of explanation from Mr Cattermole could console her.

Hannah was enjoying his discomfort. Juno went on and on about the cat, was it a ginger tom or a tabby or coal black? A white one? With one blue eye just like Jacka?

After a few minutes, Mr Cattermole mumbled something about venturing into the countryside to hire a konaki. Time was moving on. He hoped that Captain had not strayed too far in his search for fresh grass.

He walked away into the scrub, calling out to Jacka to stay boy, stay.

The dog, lying full length outside the door of the hut lifted his head then lowered it with a deep sigh. His thick winter coat covered up his emaciated body.

But he is very old thought Hannah. Why haven't I noticed this before?

She was angry and more than a little afraid. A pattern was emerging between her and Mr Cattermole. If something annoyed him, he took it for a while but then walked off.

No such luxury for her. Now that Juno was becoming noticeably pregnant she could not be left. She could barely walk. Hannah was worried.

Juno complained that she felt ill. Hannah washed her forehead with the last of the warm water from the iron kettle. A slight fever, just enough to worry her. She dried Juno's face with a flannel, the only piece of clean towelling left in Hannah's pikau.

The day wore on. Hannah was grateful that the raging easterly that had kept them inside had not returned. Mr Cattermole had warned her not to relight the fire while he was gone. He said that the wind sometimes changed direction and roared down the chimney like a blow torch. Many of these old dwellings had perished in this manner.

Mr Cattermole came back after a few hours, despondent at his failure to find a konaki. He had kept away from the public roads in case he was seen. He had skirted around the tops of rugged hillocks colonised by a few remnants of native bush that had escaped the burning of the land.

He could not raise anybody. He knocked on a few farmhouse doors but no one had answered him. The land looked blighted, neglected. On one farm, a whole hillside had slipped away leaving long ugly clay scars.

He regretted taking Captain on such a hard ride. Come what may, his horse must be rested tomorrow.

He went into the hut. Juno was asleep. Hannah opened a tin of beans awash with a dark sauce of unknown origin. Mr Cattermole spooned some beans into his mouth and immediately spat them out. 'Rancid,' he said.

Hannah asked if it was safe to light the fire now that he had returned. Juno needed the warmth. She was unwell.

He went outside to fetch some firewood. Soon, the flames made a cheerful crackle and the mood within the hut lightened.

'This is more like it,' said Mr Cattermole, sipping his mug of billy tea.

Hannah opened another tin and poured the contents into an enamel saucepan. 'Good,' she said. 'Tinned corn. Sweet as a nut.'

Juno was still asleep. Hannah did not want to wake her. She and Mr Cattermole ate the whole tin between them.

'Now for the hard stuff,' said Mr Cattermole. 'There are decisions to be made. Given that I could not find a konaki or any other conveyance, not even a broken down old nag or a decrepit pack horse, how the hell are we going to get out of here?'

'We managed with one horse before,' said Hannah. 'I am happy to walk.'

'But you said that Juno is ill. We can't put her into the saddle. She must be able to lie down.'

'Perhaps we should wait here for a while.'

Mr Cattermole frowned. 'Aren't you forgetting something? That damn doctor will soon realise that he has been made a fool of. He will come back here with a posse in tow.'

'Maybe he will let us alone now that he has seen the foetus.'

'Don't count on it. He's obsessed and that's what makes him a dangerous man.'

Hannah burst into tears. She had tried to make sense of

everything that had happened to her and Juno the past few days but had failed. Her perception of what was real and what was fantasy were becoming more and more difficult to unravel.

Mr Cattermole said he hated to see a woman cry, but Hannah could not stop. She was aware that he had taken her in his arms and was dabbing at her tears ineffectively with the flannel that she had used to wipe Juno's fever away.

Jacka came through the open door. He licked Hannah's face. She closed her eyes.

'Please stop,' said Mr Cattermole.

'I'm sorry,' said Hannah.

He stroked both sides of her face with his rough hands. She remembered how cold his skin was when he had almost drowned. Now, he was fleshy and warm and smelled of tea and tobacco.

Jacka gave an excited yelp and hobbled outside.

'Listen,' said Mr Cattermole. 'Can you hear a horse approaching?'

Hannah shook her head.

'Be careful,' said Mr Cattermole. 'It could be friend or foe.'

They crept outside. Hannah hid behind the chimney. Mr Cattermole held on to Jacka's collar. Eleanor came into view, leading a black horse dragging something behind him.

'Oh you clever woman,' said Mr Cattermole. 'Look Hannah, a konaki. At least I think that's what it is.'

Mr Cattermole inspected the small rectangular wooden box attached to the rear of the horse. It was roughly made, with wooden wheels. Hannah had once seen a similar contraption loaded up with small children that came too close to the boundary of the settlement. They were lost they said, do you know where our school is?

Mr Cattermole said the konaki was better than nothing. It would ride more smoothly if it had runners but it would do.

Eleanor looked exhausted. She asked Hannah to tether her horse. She gave a half-smile when Mr Cattermole wanted to know where the horse came from.

'Don't fuss Wilfred,' said Eleanor. 'I borrowed it. Temporarily you understand.'

Mr Cattermole ran his hands down the horse's neck. 'Look,' he said. 'Black dye.'

Hannah asked if it was safe for the horse. Eleanor said it doesn't hurt them. One good downfall of rain takes them back to their original state.

'You'll have us all in jail woman,' said Mr Cattermole. 'Now come inside and rest awhile. I'm trying to keep the fire going.'

'Where is Juno?' asked Eleanor.

'Sleeping,' said Mr Cattermole. 'She has a fever. Hannah is sorting her out.'

'Did you use any of the medicines and herbal cures in my canvas bag?'

Hannah confessed that she had peeked inside. There were some herbs there but she was afraid to give them to Juno in case they affected her unborn child.

'Well done,' said Eleanor. 'Better to let nature take its course at this late stage.'

Hannah took some oats to the black horse in a spare feed bag. Captain whinnied a greeting to the new horse. Although Hannah had not been permitted to ride at the settlement, she had some understanding of horse behaviour. She was almost certain that Captain knew the other horse and that the recognition was mutual.

She went back inside the shack where Mr Cattermole was trying to revive the fire. The damp wood spat and hissed.

'Oh for some decent puriri,' said Mr Cattermole. 'This manuka loves to spit.'

'Spit spit spit,' said Juno. She was still clutching the jar of formaldehyde with its resident floating about inside.

Eleanor sighed. 'I suppose it's too late for us to leave here tonight.'

'It would be risky,' said Mr Cattermole. 'The weather may turn nasty again. The little one would not cope.'

'In that case, I will prepare some food for tomorrow,' said Eleanor. 'Just a small loaf of soda bread again I'm afraid.'

The darkness came down suddenly. Soon, the paraffin lamp was hissing and glowing and the fire became almost too hot to bear. Mr Cattermole let Jacka in. A favour he said, for an old dog still able to work.

Eleanor kneaded the bread. She and Mr Cattermole took turns at sipping from a hip flask.

'Tipsy,' he crowed. 'Let's get tipsy.'

'Too late,' said Eleanor. 'I took the last drop.'

'Aha!' said Mr Cattermole. 'I found a bottle of rum stashed away beneath a pile of rotting slabs. I kept it for emergencies. Dunno if it's any good or not. But rum can be older than God and younger than Jesus and still be drinkable.'

'Wilfred Cattermole,' said Eleanor. 'I never thought I would hear you utter such blasphemous words.'

He laughed. He offered Hannah a sip of rum. She had never tasted alcohol before. She wanted to try it but was afraid of losing control. She heard the disapproving voices of Sarah and Augusta telling stories about fallen girls who had been introduced to the demon drink.

Eleanor said, 'Go on Hannah, it will help you to get through the night.'

The first sip almost took her head off. Mr Cattermole said

easy girl, tiny sips, that's the way to go.

Hannah had another sip and then another. It was the most extraordinary feeling. She heard a stranger speaking from within her head demanding to be heard. It grew louder and more insistent.

'Go on,' said Eleanor. 'Drink as much as you like. It will do you good.'

Hannah opened her mouth and the words poured out, a confusion of accusations, of everything that she had ever suffered in the community. All she had done was to give Mr Cattermole some air from her mouth to his and the heavens fell down into that cold green river water, leaving her stained with the accusation of necromancy, the evil practice of bringing back the dead.

She recognised the outpouring of complaint as her own voice. But it must have come across as a meaningless rant because Mr Cattermole laughed and shrugged his shoulders and Eleanor tried to give her a kiss on the cheek.

The soda bread burnt to a crisp. Hannah took it out of the colonial oven and placed it on the makeshift table.

Mr Cattermole was singing sea shanties now, off-key and raucous.

Eleanor giggled. 'Keep it clean Wilfred. There are children present.'

Hannah's head started to spin, so she went to bed early, but was too agitated to fall asleep. She was disappointed in her mother's behaviour but she did not hate her. It would have been easier if she had.

The paraffin lamp grew dim. Hannah heard Mr Cattermole confess that he was afraid for Juno's welfare. What would he do if she went into childbirth in some god-forsaken shack like this?

'Hannah would be able to cope.'

'Are you sure?'

'Like mother like daughter.' Eleanor's voice was becoming a little slurred. 'She's already taken some precautions.'

'Like what?'

Hannah opened her eyes. She saw Eleanor take something from her canvas pack and give it to Mr Cattermole. It was the Skinner mask that Hannah had uplifted from Dr Graham's medical kit.

'Chloroform,' said Eleanor. 'And here's the bottle.'

Mr Cattermole asked her where she had got it from. He did not tell her that he already knew about the Skinner mask and that he and Hannah had once used it successfully on Jacka.

'I took it from Hannah's pikau.'

Hannah could not restrain herself any longer. She stood up, almost knocking over the jar containing the foetus. 'You had no right to take things from my pikau. Who knows what Dr Graham will do if he comes back?'

'What about the fake black horse?' said Mr Cattermole.

'What horse?' said Eleanor.

'Don't play the fool with me.'

Mr Cattermole took a sip of rum and offered the flask to Hannah. She shook her head. He rolled up a cigarette and lit it with a taper from the dying fire.

'Don't fret,' said Eleanor. 'I may as well put you both out of your misery.'

Mr Cattermole took in a lungful of smoke and breathed out through his nose. 'I don't like the sound of that.'

'He gave me his horse.'

Mr Cattermole said he did not believe her. Not for a minute.

'There is no chance of Dr Graham returning,' said Eleanor. 'He is no longer a threat.'

'What have you done?' said Mr Cattermole.

'The poor man met with an accident. I tried to help but he was too far gone.'

Mr Cattermole hit the table with a closed fist. 'Stop this nonsense right now.'

'You have a short memory,' said Eleanor. 'Hannah rescued you from the river and brought you back to life. I tried to do the same thing but could not. He was too heavy.'

The paraffin lamp flickered and went out. The logs in the fireplace were slowly disintegrating into fragments of grey ash. Hannah returned to the bunk bed beside Juno. Mr Cattermole shook out his bed roll and lay down near the residual warmth of the chimney. Eleanor announced that she was going to sleep outside. The walls of the shack were closing in on her.

Juno whimpered in her sleep. Hannah touched her sister's forehead. Cool at last.

Chapter 4

It took two days and two nights to reach the rural outskirts of Raglan village. They had seen a few people travelling along the old bush tracks. Nobody seemed to recognise them except for one old man carrying a pikau and a bed roll. He asked Mr Cattermole for tobacco.

'Sorry mate,' said Mr Cattermole. 'Run out.'

The old man sat down on a fallen ponga, blocking their way. He looked dejected. 'I'm sure I've seen you somewhere before.'

'Let us pass,' said Mr Cattermole.

'You a shepherd?'

'No.'

The old man would not let it go. He claimed that he had been in a shearing gang up in the head waters of the Mangawhero River years ago with Wilfred Cattermole. How time passes, yes it was all coming back to him now. How could anyone forget such an unusual name?

'Let us pass,' said Mr Cattermole, more firmly this time.

The old man slung his pikau onto his shoulders and walked away.

Juno had remained perfectly still throughout this encounter. She lay on the konaki beneath the tattered blanket that she had taken from the shack. Jacka sat at her feet, his blue eye gleaming.

'Poor old thing,' said Eleanor. 'We could have at least offered him a piece of bread.'

'I was trying to put him off the scent. We have to be careful. Especially you, riding along on a stolen horse.'

'So you did recognise that man.'

'Sort of. He's been through some hard times, you can see it on his face.'

'I'm glad you didn't give him a cigarette,' said Eleanor. 'The tobacco pouch is almost empty. I panic when it gets this low.'

'Spoken like a true addict,' said Mr Cattermole.

He seemed to be more jovial now that the stranger had moved on. He tightened up the girth on Captain's saddle. Juno laughed when Captain pushed out his stomach and took a deep breath to make the girth looser than it should be. Mr Cattermole called him a wily old fox. He knew every trick in the book.

At the end of the first day Mr Cattermole took Hannah aside and told her that he was becoming increasingly concerned with Juno's state of health.

Hannah said she was worried too. At least they had a safe way of moving her. The konaki had been declared an unexpected little miracle by Mr Cattermole. It looked like a box on wheels but it was sturdy and Captain accepted it without too much huffing and puffing.

The rain had not ceased since they had left the settler's shack. It had not been so difficult travelling along the bush tracks. But now they were coming into cleared land, and the rain pelted down, turning the soil into mud that dragged at the wheels of the konaki.

Juno was shivering. Mr Cattermole attempted to rig a canvas sheet over her but she said it was worser because it made the rain run down her neck.

'We have to find shelter,' said Mr Cattermole. 'And once we have done that, we have to make a plan.'

The rain eased off. A thin fog began to gather around the tops of the cabbage trees. The land was not so ravaged here. The bush had begun to heal the wounds of fire and axe. But where were the settlers? Mr Cattermole said he did not understand this place anymore. He thought of himself as an experienced man of the land, but he kept losing his bearings.

'Look,' said Hannah.

Mr Cattermole reined Captain in. Eleanor followed suit with her horse.

A derelict wooden building emerged out of the fog. It had a front veranda and a rusty red roof. Some of the corrugated iron sheets were missing. Stuck on the side of the veranda was a tall room with one tiny window.

Mr Cattermole said he hoped this was not a trap.

Eleanor said it can't be, it can't be.

'What is it?' asked Hannah.

'My eyes are playing tricks on me,' said Eleanor.

The front door was open. Dead leaves littered the hall. Some of the scrim had fallen off the walls onto the floor. But once they got to the kitchen, Hannah gave a sigh of relief. There was a table and four chairs, a wood stove, an enamel sink and a leaking brass tap.

'Plonk, plonk,' said Juno.

There were some small logs stacked tidily next to the wood-burning stove. Mr Cattermole took a hatchet from his saddle bag and stripped some pieces of dried bark from a manuka log.

Eleanor shuffled her feet in drifts of dry leaves. She disappeared down the hallway.

Mr Cattermole asked Hannah if she had paper and

matches. He needed some dry paper to ignite the bark. With him and Eleanor both smokers, the supply of matches had dwindled down to almost nothing.

Hannah said that she had one match left; a white Swan vesta. She wanted to hold onto it in case of emergencies.

'Juno is the emergency, right here and now. She's trembling. She must have warmth.'

Hannah said in that case he could use her last match.

He struck the match on the top of the wood burner and one leaf caught, and soon, his breath was blowing in and out, in and out, like a pair of reverential bellows. The bark flared blue, then yellow.

Eleanor came back into the kitchen. She sat at the table with her head in her hands.

'Are you ill?' said Hannah.

'Just a headache.'

'The wood burner is starting to heat up. I could make you a drink.'

'I can't stay here, it's impossible,' said Eleanor.

Hannah unpacked damp clothes from her pikau and hung them on a pulley above the stove. She shook out the grey blanket that had shielded Juno. A large flea gorged with blood hopped onto her leg. She cracked it between her thumb nails.

Mr Cattermole said that they had no choice. From now on they had to follow his plan. 'Otherwise, we are all doomed. Look at us. A horse thief, two kidnappers, and a pregnant child.'

'You don't understand,' said Eleanor.

Mr Cattermole said of all the shelters they had chanced upon it was clearly the best. He wanted to discuss his plan before getting some food together. He rolled up a cigarette for Eleanor. 'Sorry it's down to the dregs,' he said.

Eleanor took the thin cigarette from him without speaking.

She lit it from the wood stove.

Mr Cattermole said that they were not far from Raglan village. He had a contact there, a man called Stu. He would probably give them shelter.

Hannah asked if they would be safe in the village.

'It's better to be lost in a crowd than lost in the wilderness. The important thing is to blend into the landscape. We must provide a plausible explanation for our presence. Now, Eleanor, you have lived in cities, you have been a wanderer, you will not be a problem. Except for one thing. That damned horse.'

Eleanor tossed the cigarette butt into the fire. 'I won't have him harmed.'

'What do you take me for woman?' He sounded sad rather than angry.

'Can I keep the saddle? I have never seen one so soft and beautifully made.'

Mr Cattermole said absolutely not. It was time Eleanor looked at a few stark facts. 'You will be blamed for the doctor's death if you are seen riding his horse or using any tackle that can be traced back to him. Added to this, he is well known for his attitudes towards mental defectives and if it comes out that you are shielding someone who should not be allowed to breed there will be hell to pay. It will be seen as a revenge killing.'

Eleanor said she had not harmed that wretched man. She had not tried very hard to save him either but that was another matter.

'Back to our plan,' said Mr Cattermole. 'We are going to become an ordinary family. Eleanor will be the mother, Juno will be Eleanor's last child and Hannah the first.'

'Who will you be?' asked Hannah.

Mr Cattermole paused. 'I will be your husband. The father of your child.'

Eleanor said he must be mad.

'We must hide Juno's pregnancy and her identity,' said Mr Cattermole. 'Her life depends on it.'

'But she is already showing,' said Hannah.

Eleanor said hang on a minute. It's so crazy it just might work. Rich families in Auckland had special corsets made up to conceal pregnancies that had occurred on the wrong side of the blanket. Juno could wear one of these contraptions until she gave birth.

'Where would we get one?' asked Mr Cattermole.

'I could make one out of an old corset,' said Eleanor.

'What about me?' asked Hannah.

Eleanor said she could not remember ever seeing the reverse garment. But this would be relatively easy to make with calico and sackcloth. It would look like a padded apron.

'The big question is what Juno would make of it,' said Mr Cattermole. 'Would she co-operate?'

Hannah said that Juno seemed to have a special insight into the protection of children, both born and unborn. She cares for the foetus in the jar even though she knows it is not hers.

Mr Cattermole shuddered. He said that he found the whole foetus thing macabre. He swore the damn thing watched him out of the corner of its eye. One of the first things he planned to do after they got settled in Raglan was to bury it deep in the volcanic soil of Mount Karioi.

Eleanor took out needles and scissors and bits and pieces of cloth from her canvas pack. She held up a stained corset, once pink in colour. She said it was for a much bigger lady but she could make do.

'See,' she said. 'Here are the eyelets to thread the ribbons through. The lady wraps it round her tummy and then we lace her up and pull the ribbons tight.'

'Make do, make do,' said Juno.

Mr Cattermole brought out the bottle of rum.

Hannah washed out some chipped cups that hung from hooks. She marvelled at the water tap that turned off and on so easily. She had never seen water gush so freely from a tap. She played with it until Mr Cattermole asked her to taihoa. It was making a man want to pee.

'Wilfred! Language please,' said Eleanor.

'She'd better get used to it now that she's my wife,' said Mr Cattermole sipping his way through another shot of rum.

Hannah did not mind being teased. It created a connection between her and Mr Cattermole that she found comforting. She resolved to learn how to answer back once she had got over her feelings of shyness in his presence.

'Turn around ladies, no peeking,' said Mr Cattermole. 'I'm going to play dress-up too.'

Hannah closed her eyes. When she opened them again she recognised the tweed jacket, the white shirt and the blue tie that Mr Cattermole had uplifted from her father's shop in Piopio.

Eleanor gasped. 'Where did you get that outfit? It must be worth a bob or two.'

'I got it to sell,' said Mr Cattermole.

He said he should be able to pass muster as a townie in this getup. Just one more thing to do. Get rid of his beard. He is loath to do this but until things settle down they must be careful.

He opened his pikau and took out his shaving gear. He did not have a strop to sharpen his cut-throat razor but made do with a worn leather belt. He asked Eleanor to help him.

'Not on your life,' she said. 'One slip of my shaky hands and you'll be minus a hunk of flesh.'

'Thanks for the warning.'

'Perhaps Hannah could do it,' said Eleanor.

Hannah shook her head.

Mr Cattermole said he was willing to give Hannah a go. A steady young hand and a good teacher is all that is required.

Hannah gathered herself together. She had been trained from her early teenage years to shave the men for ceremonial purposes when a virginal hand was required.

Hannah found a chipped enamel bowl under the sink. It was difficult to get the good lather going with a worn shaving brush and cold water. She added some warm water from the kettle and this helped somewhat.

'Ouch,' said Mr Cattermole. 'Wish I had a mirror.'

'Relax,' said Hannah. 'Just let me stretch the skin on your neck a little.'

Eleanor said, 'Don't worry Wilfred. She knows exactly what she's doing.'

At the end, he had to agree. He ran his hands over his cheeks and declared them to be as smooth as a baby's bum.

Hannah spent time explaining a new game to Juno. Happy families she called it. A mummy and daddy and soon a new baby. 'We'll pretend I'm having the baby instead of you.'

'Who am I then?' asked Juno.

'You are Eleanor's daughter. You are my sister and Mr Cattermole is your brother-in-law.'

'Whoa,' said Eleanor. 'Can you say it again? I'm more muddled that she is.'

Juno laughed. She thought it all a great joke. 'Will the new baby have a name?'

'Of course,' said Hannah. 'But we have to wait until it is

born. And in the meantime, you must not tell anyone our big secret.'

Eleanor threaded the last of the ribbon through the eyelets on the corset. She undressed Juno down to her camisole and bloomers. The corset fitted Juno perfectly. Eleanor tightened a ribbon. It broke and she said damn and blast beneath her breath.

'You swore,' said Juno.

'Sorry,' said Eleanor.

Mr Cattermole removed one of his shoe laces and gave it to Eleanor. She pulled the shoe lace slowly through the eyelet. It held. Eleanor sighed with relief.

Mr Cattermole got to his feet.

'Where are you going?' asked Eleanor.

Mr Cattermole said it was time to get rid of the doctor's horse. He had seen a paddock a few miles away at the side of Old Mountain Road. 'I'll tie him up and someone will soon see him and return him to the village.'

Hannah offered to go with him taking Captain and doubling up on the trip back.

Mr Cattermole said he had considered that but he did not want anyone to see Hannah just yet. They should wait until Eleanor had made the special padded outfit.

'I wish you had chosen a different horse to steal,' he said. 'Everyone will recognise the doctor's horse.'

'Go then,' said Eleanor. 'And if you chance upon any abandoned orchards or kitchen gardens, pilfer the heck out of them. My girls are starving.'

'I'll do my best,' he said.

Mr Cattermole came back empty handed. Night fell. The glow from the wood-burning stove provided some light.

Eleanor had managed to produce some wild potatoes,

small, with purplish skins and blighted eyes.

Mr Cattermole said it was clever of Eleanor to find anything at all edible. The vegetation looked terminally ill.

'I know this place,' said Eleanor. 'I came here as a girl.'

Mr Cattermole did not listen. He was full of himself and how clever he had been about the doctor's horse. He had left the horse saddled up close to the edge of Old Mountain Road as planned. The horse had stared at him for a full minute, then gave a strange cry, reared up onto his back legs, and was off like the wind.

He hesitated.

'Go on,' said Eleanor, 'what happened next?'

Mr Cattermole said there's nothing more to say. The horse was there, and then it was not.

'Good,' said Eleanor. She finished peeling the potatoes then filled a saucepan with water and placed the pot on top of the wood-burning stove.

Juno lifted her head up from the table. She asked Mr Cattermole if he had seen the horse fly up into the night sky.

Mr Cattermole smiled and called her a right little cod. But if she wanted to see a magic horse why not conjure it up now?

Juno demonstrated how to walk like a horse, tapping the ground with one delicate hoof. She waited. Nothing happened. She tried again, this time cupping both her ears with her hands. She whispered. 'Can you hear the beating of the wings? Can you hear?'

They ate the wild potatoes. Eleanor made a pot of billy tea out of some dried herbs that she had found at the bottom of her saddle bag.

Juno pushed out her lower lip. She wanted more potatoes not this scented water.

'But it's lovely,' said Eleanor. 'It's made of camomile flowers.'

Mr Cattermole said that he must go out early in the morning to forage for food. No, not rabbits, stuff from the Raglan store. Cheese and sausages and tea and flour. Real food.

Eleanor wanted to go with him but he said too soon. A few more days and then they could emerge one by one until they became part of the landscape.

'In that case,' said Eleanor, 'please bring me a pound of lard.'

'What for?'

She held out her right hand without speaking. He took her hand in his and smoothed the ragged purple scar on the back. 'Lye soap?' he asked.

'What else.'

'You don't have to battle with homemade soap any more. I'll bring you some Knights Castile from the store.'

She hesitated, then confessed that she had absolutely no money, not a skerrick. Could he set up an account in his name? She had spent the last of her wages on buying a feed bag for the stolen horse and bits and pieces of cloth for the girls.

'What was your job?'

'I was a cook at a boarding house out west of Auckland. A dubious place at the best of times.'

Hannah sat quietly throughout their interchange. She felt invisible. Was she jealous of Mr Cattermole's relationship with her mother?

I am like a child, I don't know how to be, she thought. Juno is smarter than I am. She does not need to cultivate the artifices demanded of me as an adult woman. Looking into Juno's eyes conjures up a vision of unclouded honesty whereas my eyes are forever concealing and revealing, ducking and diving at one and the same time.

She remembered the night that Abraham had called the congregation together to learn her fate after she had rescued Mr Cattermole from drowning. Abraham had read a passage aloud from the book of Samuel about the Witch of Endor, a woman known to have a familiar spirit that allows her to bring back the dead. Abraham had warned Hannah not to become a bone-conjuror, even if a king begged her service.

She remembered the cold room, the felt hats nodding in approval, her inability to speak. She remembered her determination not to cry in front of her tormentors.

She dreamed of taking her revenge on the elders. She would return to the settlement dressed in black clothes, long and dense and ragged, a tall thin hat, rings on her fingers, crushed herbs from a mortar flung about to release something from the dark arts, wild and exotic, so that everything that was once forbidden would become a game, a song of laughter and of purity.

Eleanor found a job in Raglan as a cook at the Harbour View Hotel. Hannah admired her ability to move so easily into the world of a busy hotel, where single men and family groups ate breakfasts of mutton chops and fried potato washed down with stewed tea reeking of tannin, while at the back door, the local fishermen tried to shock her with their dirty jokes when they handed over the catch of the day.

It's not so hard she said to Hannah. Just smile a lot and pretend that you have never heard anyone else say bloody hell or excuse my French before.

Hannah could feel the fabric of her old world fracturing, stitch by stitch, word by word. Some days she could swear that her stomach was beginning to swell and that something or someone was taking root inside of her.

She knew better than to mention this to Eleanor. Or Wilfred.

He had hardly spoken a word to her except to nod approvingly when she first addressed him as Wilfred. For the first two weeks after their arrival he had retreated into a whirl of activity, ripping down the scrim in the main rooms to reveal unpainted sarking held together with glue and old newspapers. His friend Stu brought building materials, most of them liberated from the local tip. He wore a black singlet, cotton drill trousers and a bowler hat. Stu said that this hat was his last link with the old country, that's why he could never take it off. It had belonged to his grandfather.

Eleanor did not have to go into the hotel on Mondays. This gave Captain a day of rest. He was the only means of transport for all of them now that the doctor's horse had been set free up on the Old Mountain Road. Sometimes Captain made the journey to and from Raglan several times a day. The konaki was parked at the back of the house just in case a passing traveller saw it and marvelled at its eccentric shape. Mr Cattermole said that after a few weeks had passed he planned to drive it into Bow Street with Juno riding in it like a queen and Jacka riding like a prince. By then the locals would know who we were, or at least they would think they did. Make no mistake, he said. The gossip is rife. One day when things settle down a bit I'll tell you some of the tall tales that have been created around our presence.

It was a warm spring day. Mr Cattermole and Stu were replacing washers and nails in the rusty roof. Their boots rattled against the loose sheets of corrugated iron. Stu was droning on with one of his long-winded monologues. Mr Cattermole punctuated the story with an occasional grunt.

Below them, Hannah and Eleanor were working in the

kitchen. Hannah was kneading bread. Eleanor was removing ashes from the firebox. She told Hannah to take Stu's stories with a pinch of salt. For one thing, he claims to know who owns this house and that he has the say of who comes and goes.

'Bet he doesn't know that this building was once a rural school,' said Eleanor. 'I came here long ago. There were only five of us. I was the tallest kid. See that little window up high? It was my job to open the window with a hook on the end of a long pole.'

She told Hannah about the time when she had misjudged the length of the pole and received a thrashing for breaking the glass. She remembered how the fragments fell slowly, riding the beams of dust like tiny opaque horses, so beautiful and yet so terrifying. She had known what would happen to her.

Hannah asked her if she wanted to find somewhere else to live, a place without the burden of past memories to cope with.

Eleanor sighed. 'Is there such a place? If so, I seemed to have used up my quota. Once that wretched wanderlust seeks me out, I have to keep moving.'

Hannah did not want her mother to leave. The thought of caring for a new-born without her help was frightening. Juno was the wild card. Would she be able to care for the baby without hurting it?

As if on cue, Juno ran into the kitchen. She wept, softly at first, then in a rising crescendo. She held up the body of a mummified mouse that had been caught between two boards in the sarking.

Mr Cattermole heard her screaming and climbed down the ladder.

Stu followed behind him at a more leisurely pace. He leaned

against the kitchen door and gave Hannah one of those conspiratorial leers beneath his disgusting hat, a look that she loathed.

Hannah could not bear that supercilious stare a moment longer. She stood up. Her padded apron caught on a rough edge of the table. She felt his eyes move down her body. He lifted his head and stared into her eyes.

She realised at once that he had guessed her secret. She wanted to run as fast as she could, away, back to the raupo hut, or the settler's cottage, even to the harsh conditions at the Christian community, anywhere but here.

She took Juno in her arms and promised that she could have a mouse all of her own, a little pet, just stay quiet and a mouse would come in a tiny cage to live with us.

'One with a little wheel?'

'Just as soon as we have finished the repairs.'

'Promise?'

'Promise.'

Days passed. Mr Cattermole said they would not see much of Stu now that the renovations were almost complete. He was due to come back next week to check up on the quality of the workmanship. Then he could give the owner of the house a satisfactory account of their deal.

Eleanor was bending over the range, stirring the porridge pot. 'What are you up to now Wilfred? Another one of your plans made without consulting us?'

'Look who's talking. You jump from one place to another. I never know where you are going to pop up next.'

Hannah wanted them to stop bickering. It made her anxious. She tried to keep her voice light. 'Would any one like a cup of tea?'

'Not me,' said Eleanor. 'Let's have this out, once and for all.'

'Good idea,' said Mr Cattermole. 'I didn't want to tell you before because Stu can be a bit of a rogue.'

Hannah braced herself. How can she tell them that Stu has guessed that she is faking her pregnancy?

Mr Cattermole said that he didn't know who owned the house. They wished to remain anonymous. 'Stu's organised it all for us, we can stay for up to a year, rent free, if we do some renovations.'

Eleanor was not satisfied. She wanted to know what was in it for Stu or the owner of the house for that matter. 'And don't give me the good-hearted neighbour run-around either.'

Mr Cattermole looked a little sheepish.

Eleanor pounced. 'You are up to something Wilfred Cattermole. And you are not leaving this kitchen until you have spilled the beans.'

Hannah's throat tightened. This is it, she thought. I am about to be unmasked.

But it was Mr Cattermole who had crossed the line. He had shared a few beers with Stu at the Harbour View Hotel and had accidentally let it slip that he and Hannah were not married even though she was pregnant. Stu nearly fell off his bar stool.

'You idiot,' said Eleanor

'I swore him to secrecy.'

'He won't take any notice of that.'

'There's something else. Don't take this the wrong way Hannah, but he told me that he is carrying a torch for you.'

Hannah could not speak. Eleanor did it for her. 'What a cheek.'

'He fancies himself as a saviour of the fallen,' said Mr Cattermole.

Eleanor ladled hot oatmeal into the bowls. 'Well, at least he bought the pregnancy thing. Imagine what he would do if he found out about Juno.'

Juno wandered into the kitchen, carrying the jar where the foetus lived. She was fed up. There was something inside her playing hidegoseek. She had told it to go away but it just gets worser.

Eleanor said it will all be over in a few weeks. Mr Cattermole was surprised. So soon, he said. Was she sure? Eleanor said it is a little difficult given how tiny she is. The baby is tiny too. And the poor little thing is lying sideways. I hope and pray that the head comes down before she goes into labour.

Mr Cattermole frowned. 'Tell me when it starts happening. I don't want to be here.'

Eleanor whispered 'coward' under her breath.

'No, not true,' said Mr Cattermole. 'I have become fond of the child in spite of her strange behaviour. I would hate to see her distressed and in pain.'

Juno spooned some oatmeal into her mouth.

Mr Cattermole asked if Juno would like to come into Raglan this morning. 'Yes, in the konaki. It is already common knowledge that there are women living here. Tongues are wagging. Time to put a face to the gossip. And it would be a good outing for Juno. Poor girl is coming down with cabin fever if you ask me.'

'I already knew that you're an idiot, but this takes the cake,' said Eleanor.

But Mr Cattermole had struck a nerve. Juno, then Hannah, begged him to take them into the village. He said that he would have to take them one at a time. And Jacka has to come too. He does not like to be parted from me.

Jacka opened one blue eye, then the brown. He sighed.

'Right, let's make a move,' said Mr Cattermole. He went off to catch Captain who was grazing in a paddock next to the old school house.

Hannah helped Juno to dress. Juno whimpered a little when Hannah tied the corset.

'Be brave,' said Hannah. 'Not much longer to wait.'

There was a commotion in the kitchen. The dog gave out a half-hearted warning bark. Hannah told Juno to wait in the bedroom. She went into the kitchen. There was a policeman on the porch leaning through the window.

'Go and get Wilfred,' said Eleanor.

Mr Cattermole was attempting to catch the wily Captain. The horse had no intention of leaving his succulent patch of grass to pull a rattling konaki along a muddy road. He allowed Mr Cattermole to come close, and then took off again.

He heard Hannah calling his name. 'Wilfred come quickly.'

'What's going on?'

'A policeman is here. You must come.'

They ran back to the house.

Eleanor was waiting for them in the kitchen with the news that the missing doctor had been found. 'Or what's left of him. Fell off his horse and drowned by the looks of it.'

'Good God,' said Mr Cattermole.

Hannah sat down on a kitchen chair. She had never seen a policeman before. She was terrified. What was she supposed to do? She wanted to rip off her padded apron, confess all, but a warning look from Mr Cattermole stopped her.

The policeman, who had travelled out from Hamilton the day before in a motor car, complained about the state of Old Mountain Road. Slips all over the place. Two flat tyres. He would much rather have ridden his horse.

He wrote a few notes in a dog-eared notebook. He

scratched his head. 'The good Doctor met his death by drowning in a tributary of the Mokau.'

'What's it got to do with us?' asked Mr Cattermole.

'There's just one problem. He would have survived if he had not had his hands tied behind him.'

'So it's murder?'

'Early days yet. We are checking out everyone who was at a meeting of the local eugenics society at Cooper's shop at Piopio about seven weeks ago. There were some heated arguments about what to do with a pregnant mental defective who was under the care of Doctor Graham. I understand you were there.'

Mr Cattermole frowned. 'Can't remember that far back.'

The policeman closed his notebook and placed it in his pocket. 'Perhaps if you recall anything you could stop in at my new office in Raglan.'

Eleanor invited him into the kitchen to take a cup of hot tea with them. Has he eaten? There is plenty of porridge left.

He loaded up the bowl with sugar and milk and demolished the rest of the porridge. Soon he was chatting away with Mr Cattermole as if he had known him for years. How does the missus cope with the isolation and the danger of this blighted place? The black sand ever shifting, the roar of the tide breaking over the bar, that cursed southerly that cuts right through you like a knife.

Hannah excused herself and went into the bedroom she shared with Juno. She saw a foot sticking out from under the makeshift bed. She bent down and whispered keep very still. Make no noise.

Juno put both hands out and clung to Hannah's padded apron. Her eyes were swollen with unshed tears.

Eleanor called from the kitchen, 'Where are you? Constable

Mills is going now.'

Hannah stayed behind the door praying that Eleanor would not bring their unwelcome visitor down the hall. She closed the door softly. Except for one tiny muffled sob, Juno did not make a sound.

Hannah went back to the kitchen.

'Cheer up girls, it's all over,' said Mr Cattermole.

But Hannah could not stop trembling. She felt as if she was standing at the edge of a cliff in the centre of a waterfall that was about to push her down to the rapids below. Did her mother tie the doctor's wrists together? Was Eleanor the only witness to the accident? If not, what really happened?

Eleanor said she had ridden the doctor's horse too hard. Perhaps it had cantered back to the river to find his master.

Mr Cattermole said you are mistaken. It's the wrong horse. There would not be enough time for it to get back to the river.

'Please stop,' pleaded Hannah.

She went back into the bedroom. Juno had come out from under the makeshift bed. She looked frightened. She opened her hands. Blood dripped from her fingers.

Hannah called out to Eleanor. 'Come quickly, it's started.'

Eleanor came running. Hannah showed her the blood on Juno's hands.

'I wet my pants, I didn't mean to,' said Juno.

'Hop on the bed my darling,' said Eleanor. 'Let me have a look.'

Hannah sorted through the objects in her pikau. She removed the flannel cover from the Skinner mask and unfolded the wire frame. The bottle of chloroform was securely corked; she was ready.

'Oh you are a clever girl Juno,' said Eleanor. 'The baby has turned around, the head is engaged. You have bled a little.

Nothing to worry about.'

'But it's too early,' said Hannah.

'That may be a good thing. She could never carry a large baby.'

Mr Cattermole appeared at the door. 'Is everything all right?'

'Go,' said Eleanor.

He looked relieved. 'I'm off to Raglan to pick up supplies. That's if Captain will allow me to catch him.'

'Just go,' said Eleanor.

Eleanor took a few objects from her pikau and laid them out; a pot of herbal ointment, aspirin tablets and a special knife to cut the cord. She asked Hannah to bring some towels from the clothes hoist in the kitchen. They were in tatters, but clean.

'Have you done much birthing?'

'Hundreds, and never lost one yet.'

Hannah knew that she was lying. She saw her mother cross her fingers behind her back.

'How many?' she whispered.

Eleanor held up three fingers.

Hannah was shocked. She asked Eleanor if there were any midwives in the district. Eleanor said she didn't know. Nobody at the hotel where she worked ever mentioned it. Not that this meant anything. It was a taboo subject even if you were married. And now that Doctor Graham had passed away there was no one else. He was useless anyway, too far away to help, and if he did arrive on time, he was usually half cut.

'How do the Māori women get on?'

'They have their own methods,' said Eleanor. 'Most of the time they do just fine.'

'Would they help us if we asked?'

'Of course,' said Eleanor. 'But aren't you forgetting something? You are the one meant to be giving birth to a baby, not Juno.'

Hannah removed her padded apron. 'It has almost become a part of me. I'll miss it.'

Juno began a wail that started low and ended on a high note, pure and quivering, like the call of the bell bird. It came and peaked and fell back into the deep recesses of her body.

Soon the wail came every few minutes. Hannah could not hold back her tears.

'Don't frighten her,' said Eleanor.

'I'm trying.'

'I can't believe how quickly she is progressing,' said Eleanor.

'When should we use the mask?'

'Soon, but we must be careful to use a small amount. If she is deeply unconscious she will stop pushing.'

Hannah placed three drops of chloroform onto the mask and placed it over her sister's face.

'Juno, you must push when I tell you to,' said Eleanor. 'Do you understand?'

Juno did not respond.

'I only used three drops,' said Hannah. Her voice was shaking.

Eleanor admitted that she too was in uncertain territory, but in spite of their fear, they decided to keep Juno at a minimal level of consciousness.

The contractions still came but they seemed to be weaker and less frequent. Then, just as they were ready to give up on the chloroform, Juno let out a wail that seemed to have no end. On and on it went, louder and higher, feral, like the death throes of a wild animal.

'The head is almost there,' said Eleanor. 'Quick, get behind her, hold her shoulders up.'

Hannah obeyed. Eleanor said push now and Juno did, taking big breaths. The child catapulted into Eleanor's arms.

'It's a girl, a little girl,' said Hannah.

Juno closed her eyes. Eleanor cut the cord. She massaged Juno's abdomen and retrieved the afterbirth.

There was little blood. Hannah washed the inert body of her sister. She asked Eleanor if this was normal. Surely there would be some damage to attend to. The women back at the community spoke of the stitching required after childbirth. It almost became a state of honour to count up the stitches, those great black knots of animal gut piercing that most tender of places.

Eleanor said she had never seen anyone give birth so easily. She was elated, relieved. She could jump to the moon and back.

Hannah packed the Skinner mask and the bottle of chloroform away. She hoped that she would never have to use it again.

Eleanor said amen to that.

Hannah heard a horse approaching the house. It was Mr Cattermole returning from Raglan. He walked up the rotting steps of the veranda and scuffed his boots on the shoe-scraper.

Hannah called out to him. 'It's safe to come inside now.'

'Is it all over?' he whispered.' He was still scraping his shoes as if his life depended upon it.

'A tiny girl, very small.'

They went into the kitchen. Eleanor was busily lining a small cardboard box with wads of cotton wool.

Mr Cattermole stared at the tiny baby.

'Don't stand there like a headless chook,' said Eleanor.

'What's the cotton wool for?'

'To keep her clean and warm.'

The night came down. Hannah was worried about Juno. She was still lying on Eleanor's bed. Her breath was shallow and her eyes were shut.

Eleanor said not to worry. There was little blood. This was a good sign. The baby had changed in colour from pale blue to a healthy pink. When she cried she sounded like a mewling kitten.

Juno sat up suddenly and called out to Hannah. 'Where are you? I'm starving.'

Hannah helped her into the kitchen. Juno ignored the mewling sound coming from the cardboard box.

'It's alright Juno,' said Hannah. 'No more pain. The little baby has come out of you. See how tiny her fingernails are.'

Juno did not answer. She was busily unwrapping some of the food packets that Mr Cattermole had brought back from Raglan.

Hannah asked Juno if she had chosen a name for the baby yet.

Juno, her mouth full of broken biscuits, shook her head. She wanted to know where the real baby was. The one who floated in the big glass jar.

'She's getting confused,' said Mr Cattermole.

'She's trying to make sense of what has happened to her,' said Eleanor. 'She has no memory of what she has just been through. It is kinder to agree with her.'

Mr Cattermole asked Hannah to give Juno some chocolate from his pikau, then take her back to Eleanor's room. He wanted to speak to Eleanor. Alone.

Hannah hesitated. She did not want to be left out of what was clearly going to be an important conversation.

Eleanor said off you go before I get stuck into that

chocolate myself.'

Hannah helped Juno onto the bed. She broke the chocolate into neat squares. Juno wolfed her portion down then asked for more. Hannah handed over what was left of the block, leaving one tiny square for herself.

She left Juno where she was and crept along the hall. She could hear Mr Cattermole's voice clearly. He was laying down the law about Eleanor staying put instead of doing one of her infamous disappearing acts.

Hannah could not hear her mother's answer. She gave up and walked back into the kitchen.

'I knew you were listening,' said Mr Cattermole. 'I heard the floor boards creak.'

Eleanor created a diversion by lifting the baby from the box. She claimed to be suffering from a deep sense of fatigue. She said that it was all very well for you young people. But if she doesn't get some sleep soon she'll fall over.

'There is unfinished business between us,' said Mr Cattermole.

'What do I have to do to make you believe me?'

'Because when I look back on your past life there are patterns, disturbing ones.'

Hannah took the baby from Eleanor. She asked if the baby should be fed. If so, how would they do it?

'Look in my pikau,' said Mr Cattermole. 'I bought two glass bottles, a rubber teat, and a packet of dried milk powder.'

Eleanor said that the cow's milk would be too strong. Sugar and water for the first few days would do the trick.

Eleanor poured hot water over the rubber teat. Then she poked two small needle-holes into the top. 'Just enough flow to feed the child without choking her,' she said.

Mr Cattermole said it was a good thing that Eleanor was

here. What did he know about such things?

'You brought the right feeding equipment,' she said.

'The grocer's wife helped me out.'

'You fool. She will spread it all around Raglan.'

'It doesn't matter,' said Mr Cattermole. 'As far as she knows it's Hannah who has given birth.'

'Can I feed her?' asked Hannah.

Eleanor said yes but test the water on your forearm first. It has to be the same temperature as blood. Add a pinch of sugar. Jiggle the bottle to make sure the sugar is dissolved. Tap her cheek with the teat. She will turn her head to find it.

The baby drank some of the sweet water, just a little but enough to make Eleanor smile.

Hannah patted the baby's back and was rewarded with a tiny bubble of wind.

'A good sign,' said Eleanor. 'Most babies take days or weeks to learn that.'

Juno came into the kitchen. She looked refreshed. No one could have guessed that she had just given birth. She wanted more chocolate. The little baby was hungry.

Hannah tried to change the subject but Juno would not let her. She went on and on about the chocolate and the baby in the jar.

Mr Cattermole snapped. 'For god's sake would somebody shut her up.'

Juno began to sob. She was inconsolable.

'See what you've done?' said Eleanor. 'Why don't you collect your stuff and go somewhere else for a while.'

Jacka hobbled into the kitchen. He flopped down beneath the table.

Mr Cattermole stroked Jacka. He withdrew his hand. It was streaked with blood.

'Oh my god,' said Eleanor.

Mr Cattermole pulled his dog out from the table by the collar. There was blood around his muzzle.

'Oh my god,' said Eleanor again.

'What's wrong?' asked Hannah.

Eleanor sat down slowly. She confessed that she could not remember where she had left the afterbirth. She had wrapped it in a towel. Could the dog have taken it away?

'Whew,' said Mr Cattermole. 'For one horrific moment I thought Jacka had been worrying a sheep.'

Eleanor said it was disgusting. How could Jacka do such a thing?

Mr Cattermole offered to take the dog away and give him a wash.

'I don't care what you do, just get that cannibal out of here,' said Eleanor.

'I'm leaving,' said Mr Cattermole. 'This place is turning into a bloody madhouse.'

'Go then,' said Eleanor.

He stomped down the front veranda. They could hear him calling out to his horse.

'Go outside Hannah,' said Eleanor. 'Be nice to him. Ask him to leave Captain here until we get on our feet.'

Hannah could not believe what her mother was asking her to do. She had been rude to Mr Cattermole and now she wanted Hannah to patch things up.

'Give me the baby,' said Eleanor. 'Quickly, before he takes off for good.'

'I won't do it,' she said.

'But we need the horse for me to get to work.'

'You should have thought of that.'

Juno lifted her head. Her face was swollen with tears. 'Are

we going now?'

'See what you have done?' said Hannah. 'She thinks we have to be on the move again.'

Eleanor said she was guilty as charged. She rambled on, going back over her life and her broken love affairs. Too late now. Her time was almost over. 'But not for you. I've seen the way that Wilfred looks at you. Not to mention Stu.'

Hannah placed the sleeping infant into the box. She had no interest in discussing these men through the framework of Eleanor's clouded past. Especially Wilfred.

'You're doing it wrong,' said Eleanor. 'You must cover the child in clean cotton wool and then swaddle her securely with a flannelette square.'

Hannah obeyed. She did not want to alienate Eleanor any further.

'I know a thing or two about babies,' said Eleanor. She lowered her voice. 'It will probably die. Too small, and too premature. So many children have died in this blighted place. Scarletina, fever, the flu, measles, diphtheria, on it goes.'

Hannah said we must do our best to protect her.

Eleanor put her arms around Hannah and gave her a hug.

The baby snuffled in her box. Juno went to sleep with her head on the table. Hannah made a pot of billy tea. Eleanor rolled up a cigarette and lit it from the stove.

They sat in companionable silence. Outside, a soft rain began to fall.

After Mr Cattermole disappeared, a routine of sorts became established at the old school house. Hannah took over the care of the baby. The baby, now named Stella, was washed and fed as often as she desired. Soon she was off the sugar water and on to milk powder.

Juno copied Hannah's every movement. She pretended to feed the foetus through the glass. She patted the bottle, brought up its wind and wrapped a cloth around it.

Hannah did not mind this parroting behaviour. It kept Juno occupied.

Eleanor made a flax basket with shoulder straps and lined it with soft cloth for Stella to ride in. Juno demanded one too.

Eleanor left the house each day except Monday morning to work at the Harbour View Hotel. Stu lent her a horse and replaced the runners of their konaki with two rusty bicycle wheels.

On her day off, Eleanor loaded Juno and Stella into the konaki behind the horse and took them into Raglan to buy groceries. People stared at the strange ménage; the new cook from the Harbour View Hotel, and an odd-looking girl with a baby swaddled in flannelette under each arm.

Hannah stayed at the house while the others were away. She imagined seeing Wilfred come into the kitchen and sit in his chair with his boots unlaced. She asked him why he had left them. Had he forgotten that she had saved him from the river?

But he never came.

Hannah and Eleanor heard rumours about the whereabouts of Wilfred. Someone saw him galloping on a black horse down Bow Street. Or was it a white one? He was possibly seen swimming underneath the Opotoru Bridge on an outgoing tide. The encounters were brief, just a flip of a fin, a quick turn of the head, and then a dimming-down of dusk falling at the edge of the night tide.

Another week passed. Eleanor and Juno had broken the ice with their trips into the village. Ladies in long dresses and sensible shoes called out to Juno, how are you today little sister? Once a church lady came running out of her doorway to give Juno a slice of fruit cake in a paper bag.

Juno, schooled by Eleanor to be distant and polite when they were in public, thanked her with dignity. The church lady peered into the konaki but saw nothing except two flannelette bundles.

Eleanor tethered the horse to the railing at the bottom of Bow Street. A familiar face loomed up behind her.

'The very woman I want to speak to,' said Constable Mills.

The policeman directed her to a tiny house at the corner of Bow Street and Wallis Street.

She was reluctant to follow him. She had not noticed the building before.

'My new office,' he said. 'It came by sea so it is a little battered,' he said.

She checked to see if Juno and Stella were secure within the konaki. Both were fast asleep. She followed Constable Mills up the wooden steps and into the two-roomed cottage.

There was a man sitting on a cane chair. He took off his leather hat and stood up. It was Mr Cooper.

'Here we are then,' said Constable Mills.

Mr Cooper stared at Eleanor. 'How long has it been? You are much changed.'

'You haven't.'

The policeman asked Mr Cooper if he wanted to have the names of his daughters taken from the missing persons file. Mr Cooper said that would be a good idea.

The constable said he did not require any further information about the death of Doctor Graham. An old woman had confessed on her deathbed. She died soon after. 'We'll never know why she did it.'

'All over and done with then,' said Eleanor.

'Not quite,' said Mr Cooper. 'There is still the problem of

Juno.'

Constable Mills looked uneasy. 'That is not a police matter.'

Eleanor heard Stella crying. She ran down the wooden steps to the edge of the road. Both the konaki and the horse had disappeared. She heard a snicker across the other side of the bridge. The mare had found some bull kelp at the waters edge and was sticking her nose into the glistening brown fronds. She licked the salt from her tongue.

Eleanor walked as fast as she could across the bridge. How did the horse get to this side of the stream? The bridge was narrow and some of the planks were missing.

She knew that it was no use to go looking for the konaki. Juno had either hidden it or someone had taken it from her.

She stayed on the back roads. She could not ride the horse. The poor creature had thrown a shoe on the ride into Raglan.

Eleanor arrived back at the old school house. Hannah was baking. There was an aroma of hot crusty bread permeating the kitchen.

Eleanor sat down heavily. 'I lost the girls.'

'But they are here,' said Hannah. 'Playing outside with Jacka.'

'How the hell did that dog get here?'

'Wilfred brought him.' She took the bread tins out of the range and tapped them on the bottom. 'He's gone now. He said a storm's coming.'

'He had no right to come back here,' said Eleanor.

Hannah said she was not sure if he meant a storm, or some other catastrophic event. 'He said that Jacka will send us a warning and that we should stay close to the house.'

Juno arrived at the kitchen door carrying Stella wrapped in a flannelette square. 'She smiled at me, she smiled!'

Hannah asked her where the other baby was.

'It died. I took it out of the jar and buried it in a sand dune.'

Hannah gasped.

Eleanor asked Juno if she would do the same thing to Stella.

'Of course not. Only dead things get buried.'

Hannah felt a surge of hope. Juno had made a logical statement. Perhaps the recent events had forced her to leave her fantasy world behind. Even if it were just a tiny light flashing in the darkness, fickle, unsubstantiated, it was there to be mined.

Jacka came hobbling into the kitchen. He threw himself beneath the table. He lifted his muzzle and howled like a wolf. On and on he went, the top notes almost disappearing in a realm of sound too high for humans to hear.

Hannah could stand it no longer. She tried to grab him by the scruff of his neck but even in his weakened state he was too strong for her.

He stopped at last. His blue eye glittered with moisture. He looked as if he was on the brink of tears.

Juno wanted to know if dogs were allowed to cry.

They ate bread together. The sun dimmed and dipped below the darkening horizon. The moon had yet to make an appearance.

At first the noise came from far away; a light tiptoe playing around the tops of the hills. The noise gathered velocity into an immense wall of sound. Within a second, the earth was tearing itself apart. Boulders rolled and branches snapped like pistol shots.

Eleanor pulled Juno and the baby underneath the table. She tried to say earthquake, earthquake, but her throat was constricted with fear. She let out a high-pitched squawk.

Hannah said don't be afraid, it will stop in a few seconds.

But it didn't. The house swayed; it jumped up and down, it rocked from side to side.

The noise died away.

Hannah crawled to the window. It was still in one piece.

The kitchen floor was littered with broken glass and tinned food, flour and potatoes, a leg of corned beef, a crust of bread.

'We must leave,' said Eleanor. 'Is the roof still on?'

Jacka crawled out from beneath the table.

'Follow the dog,' said Hannah.

The land shook and trembled.

They left the house through the back door. Jacka led them towards a rise in the paddock at the edge of the regenerating bush.

Stella began to cry in that heart-broken voice of a new-born. Eleanor tried to comfort her but she was hungry and nothing could console her.

Eleanor handed her to Hannah. 'Keep following Jacka. I'll go back to the house to find something for Stella to eat.'

The dog picked up his speed once Eleanor had gone.

They reached a clearing close to the sand dunes of Ngarimu beach. Jacka dropped to the ground, panting. Hannah tried to get her bearings. Something was wrong with the sea. Where was the bar?

The full moon lit up rivulets on the floor of the rapidly emptying harbour. Hannah shivered. She heard the voices of village people at the base of the cliff. Some of them were laughing, some were gathering shellfish, some carried torches and small nets.

A man riding on a horse was calling out to the others to get off the beach.

The water retreated even further. The horizon disappeared. Hannah could see the waves of sea grass and the black rocks and the flapping of dying fish. A wrecked boat revealed its last resting place in the deep black sand.

Hannah said they should go back. Eleanor will be worried.

'Not yet,' said Juno. 'This is where the pretend baby is buried.'

Hannah held her hand. 'Come on then, but we must be quick.'

They began to climb down the steep sand dune. A gentle breeze touched their bare faces.

Off shore, the sea began to turn. Hannah sensed its presence before she saw it.

She yelled as loudly as she could, tidal wave tidal wave! But no one on the beach paid her any attention. The man on the horse had gone.

There was a church bell ringing somewhere close to the town.

They got to the top of the dune. Juno wanted to wait and see the big wave but Hannah said no we must get back to the house. They need us.

The moon covered its face with a shroud. The wave gathered up its strength. Darkness came. The bell rang frantically, then stopped.

Hannah and Juno ran back to the school house. It was a difficult task. The terrain had altered. There were fissures across the paddocks, some of them too deep to traverse. They saw an injured horse pinned beneath a boulder. It was Captain. His eyes were dull.

'Please help him,' said Juno.

'We must keep going,' said Hannah. 'We have no choice.'

They reached the outlying creek that ran through the regenerating bush at the back of the paddock. They could hear the water coming up behind them, silently, smoothly, like an eel uncoiling itself after a long sleep.

By the time they reached the house the water was lapping at the bottom step.

Eleanor cried out from the kitchen, 'Thank god you're safe.'

'The wave will take everything,' said Hannah. 'It's a monster.'

Juno ran to the window. She rubbed a peephole in the condensation. 'The water is running away.'

'It may come back,' said Eleanor.

A gunshot rang out. Juno screamed.

'Go and have a look,' said Eleanor. She lit a paraffin lamp. 'Take this, and be careful.'

Hannah took the lamp. It burned brightly in the still air.

She found Mr Cattermole holding a shotgun. He had put Captain out of his misery. Tears ran down his unshaven face. He asked Hannah if the others were all right. Is the house damaged?

Hannah told him that the earthquake had rattled the weatherboards and tipped the table over. It was like a wild beast.

Mr Cattermole asked her if the roof was intact.

She hesitated. 'I didn't look.'

They walked back to the house. Mr Cattermole carried the gun and the saddle. Hannah carried the lantern.

'Is Eleanor still angry with me?' said Mr Cattermole.

Hannah said she had no idea.

Mr Cattermole stared at the house. It appeared to be barely touched by the earthquake. All had changed, except for this house. If he had not seen it with his own eyes he would not have believed it.

'Well well the traveller returns,' said Eleanor.

They sorted out the kitchen furniture. Apart from the spoiled food there was little damage. The fire in the stove burned brightly. Hannah found a bag of flour and made hot scones washed down with cups of billy tea.

Stella flashed her toothless smile and waved her tiny fingers.

Aftershocks rattled the house. Each time they looked at each other with a question. Is this another big shake?

Juno cried out with each rumble. She held her hands over her eyes. She wept.

Hannah remembered a childhood trick that usually worked to keep Juno calm during a thunder storm. She took an iron pan down from the rack and gave it to Juno. She found a wooden spoon to use as a drum stick. When the next aftershock came, Juno hit the pan and yelled out go away go away! The others joined in hitting and rattling anything they could find. Her tears soon turned to laughter.

Hannah saw ghostlike figures draped in blankets and woollen hats appearing through the mist. Juno was frightened. Were these the old people who disturbed her dreams?

'No,' said Hannah. 'They are from the village. Their houses are damaged.'

Juno was not convinced. Hannah said that she must be careful. If anyone asks about Stella tell them that she is my baby.

Hannah called out to the waifs and strays to come inside for tea and scones. 'Never mind the aftershocks,' she said. 'You are safe here.'

The house stretched and rocked. Someone with a deep voice started to sing a hymn. Others joined in. By late afternoon the people had drifted away. Eleanor gave each person a chunk of bread and a slice of cheese to take with them.

Night fell. When they had finished their meagre meal, Hannah turned the lamp off to conserve fuel.

Juno wanted the light back on again.

'The sun will come back in the morning,' said Hannah. 'It always does.'

'Promise?'

'Promise.'

OTHER BOOKS FROM SPINIFEX PRESS

The Word Burners
Beryl Fletcher

1992 Winner, Commonwealth Writers Prize, Best First Book, SE Asia & South Pacific

How do you decide to live? Or do others make that decision for you? In this lyrical novel, Beryl Fletcher explores the paradoxes of modern life. As a new academic, Julia finds her beliefs challenged by her students, reinforced by her friend's mistreatment and dismissed by her family. Just as her mother sought freedom from her family's rural poverty, Julia and her sister Isobel search for their own solace, finding it in different and disparate places.

> *In* The Word Burners, *Beryl Fletcher writes ordinary people with extraordinary style, revealing sisterhood in all its incarnations – blood, friendship, family, love – with pinpoint accuracy for the pain and a poignant hope for the possible.*
>
> – Stella Duffy

Rights: World
ISBN: 9781876756239
eBook: available

The Bloodwood Clan
Beryl Fletcher

When Josie is sent to Digger Town to conduct her doctoral research, she knows it is a strange place with a strange history. There, the people use no modern technologies, wear nineteenth-century clothing, drive nothing faster than a horse-and-cart, and hand-make all their goods. Even so, she is not prepared for what she finds. An intriguing tale of secrecy, politics and religious and racial intolerance.

> The Bloodwood Clan *is a sociological thriller in which [Fletcher's] growing experience as a writer is obvious in the tight pace of the narrative and all that is left unsaid.*
> – Margie Thomson
> *Weekend Herald*

Rights: World
ISBN: 9781875559800
eBook: available

The House at Karamu
Beryl Fletcher

What does a place mean? An old kauri villa with a one-roomed school attached is the place that has sustained a writer, Beryl Fletcher, through turbulent years and an obsessive love. Sent away at the age of six for a few months to the house at Karamu, she discovered books and spent many nights reading by candlelight, listening to the call of the moreporks. Karamu became a symbolic landscape of safety that helped her to survive.

> *This memoir is patient with the past – how many writers have equanimity to dwell on a previous generation's troubles as Fletcher does here? It's a tough and profoundly moving recollection of 20th-century survival as an antipodean woman and artist. Not a manifesto exactly but so illuminating and true as to have the same effect.*
>
> – Catherine Ford
> *The Age*

Rights: World
ISBN: 9781876756352
eBook: available

If you would like to know more about Spinifex Press
write for a free catalogue or visit our website

SPINIFEX PRESS
PO Box 212 North Melbourne
Victoria 3051 Australia
www.spinifexpress.com.au